DARCY'S WINTER BALL

A PRIDE AND PREJUDICE VARIATION

A.J. WOODS

Cover design by J.R. Woods

Cover image *Courtship* by Edmund Blair Leighton (1903) {{PD-US-expired}}

A.J. Woods can be found on Facebook @AuthorAJWoods

Join A.J.'s newsletter to stay updated on new book releases.

�֍ Created with Vellum

CHAPTER 1

London – December 1811

In all her life, Elizabeth Bennet had never seen so many books in one place. And it was possible, given her current situation, that she had also never in her life experienced such unguarded delight. For she was absolutely surrounded by volumes of every variety and size.

"Dearest Jane," Elizabeth said to her elder sister, who stood beside her upon entering number 173 Piccadilly, "I believe this event may be cause enough for my first case of the vapors. Should my feet rise above my head, it will be most unfortunate that Mama is not here to ply me back to consciousness with her smelling salts."

Jane Bennet giggled sweetly, as she did all things. "It would be unfortunate indeed. Let's not allow such a thing to happen. As a precaution, I shall hold fast to your arm while we browse."

Jane offered her elbow, which Elizabeth accepted, and they strolled further into Hatchards Bookshop.

"Where will we begin, Lizzy?" Jane asked with wide, wandering eyes. "In the history section, I should imagine."

"Do you not wish to start over there?" Elizabeth countered, indicating a section nearby.

Jane followed Elizabeth's direction and squinted. "But I cannot even read from here what sort of books it houses."

"It does not matter," Elizabeth said, grinning, "as they are closest to the fire."

"Oh, Lizzy," Jane scolded gently before giving in. "Alright, but we can stay only a moment. We must collect your research and then begin the journey back to our uncle's home if we are to arrive in time for tea."

"I suppose you are right," Elizabeth said, and the sisters hurried toward the large fireplace, choosing to warm their gloved hands while standing rather than taking one of the comfortable-looking chairs, inviting though they were. For Jane was correct—there was work to be done and not a great deal of time in which to accomplish it.

The two women had arrived at Gracechurch Street, where their uncle and aunt resided, shortly after dear Jane had her heart broken by a gentleman called Mr. Bingley. Though she would not reveal as much to her sister, Elizabeth herself had all but suggested the invitation to her gracious and likeminded aunt, hoping some time away from their home at Longbourn would serve as a balm to what was surely among the kindest hearts alive. And she longed to see Jane's good humor restored, almost as much as she resented the cause of its absence.

But Elizabeth would no longer dwell on past events,

and instead vowed to count her blessings more often that Mr. Bingley, his sisters, and a very particular friend of his were most certainly far, far away. After all, Christmastide was over, and the harshest stretch of winter had set in; the London streets were sparsely populated as many fashionable families had retreated to spend the season in the countryside.

She was once again consoled by the knowledge that the chance of the two eldest Bennet sisters meeting again with Mr. Bingley or Mr. Darcy were comparable to those of Jane or herself receiving a marriage proposal from a duke.

That is to say—very unlikely.

Elizabeth breathed a sigh of relief. "Come, Jane," she said, rubbing her hands together once more before leaving the fire's warmth. "Let us make our way to the geography section. There is a question of distance I must sort out if I am to get my characters to their ship on time, and the solution requires a map of the Bay of Bengal."

"Oh, Lizzy, they must make it! I cannot bear it if Thomas and Meera are unable to escape," Jane pleaded.

It was their most guarded secret, hers and Jane's.

Elizabeth had begun the serious work of composing a novel just after their father had recovered from a recent cold—short-lived but nonetheless severe. His brush with death had caused much distress among Mr. Bennet's wife and five daughters as, upon his eventual demise, their home and provision were entailed to his cousin, and the women would be left destitute thereafter but for the hope of familial charity.

After their father's health had fortunately improved,

Elizabeth's three younger sisters had all but forgotten that fear, but Jane and Elizabeth could not, and the two had begun planning how to provide for the rest—God forbid—should he not be so fortunate a second time.

Though they had a fair number of accomplishments between them, none were the sort that could be counted upon to earn an income. It was only their shared love of books that gave Elizabeth the idea that, by contributing to the increasingly popular selection of novels available, she might be able to provide for her mother and siblings in a way that would not compromise her family's station. What had begun as perhaps a foolish whim—bits of story Elizabeth had scribbled down over the years, on rainy days when diversion was scarce—was now a growing stack of paper which she believed might be of help should the very worst come to pass.

"You are too kind, dear sister," Elizabeth answered, though in truth her heart swelled with pride that Jane possessed such affection for her writing. "I fear other readers will not care for it as you do. Our sisterly bond influences your view of my work."

"I do not agree," Jane said, clasping her hands together before her chest. "I only wish you did not need a nom de plume under which to publish. Would that all of England could know the true creator of my beloved Thomas and Meera."

"I confess I share your wish," Elizabeth said quietly. "And perhaps in time I will be at liberty to declare ownership of my work, if it is indeed published in the first instance."

"It will be," Jane said, squeezing her sister's elbow. "I

know it as surely as I know my admiration of it. Now, let us find that volume you seek."

After inquiring after the location of the geography section, Jane and Elizabeth ventured up a spiral staircase until they landed at the correct floor. Jane spotted the area where the latest poetry was on display and went to browse, promising to return shortly. And when she was certain no other customers were in view, Elizabeth located the book of maps she sought, retrieved a very small notebook and pencil from her reticule, and began writing down the facts her manuscript lacked, confident that the specific details would add authenticity to her story.

Her Uncle Gardiner's library in Cheapside, though quite satisfactory, did not contain the particulars she needed for her own book. And, though at one time she might have done so—considering recent events at Longbourn—Elizabeth could not justify the expense of buying the book for herself when what she needed might be gleaned from a single page; nor could she in good conscience purchase a membership to a circulating library when she and Jane would be in London no more than a month's time. On each occasion she received it, Elizabeth carefully tucked away her pin money, just in case there came a day when her mother and sisters might need it.

This is the best way, she reassured herself, jotting down a few more lines before she closed the thick leather cover and replaced the book in its spot on the shelf.

Satisfied that the errand had been worth the journey despite the threat of snow to come, and looking forward to the warm tea that would greet them on their arrival back at Gardiner House, Elizabeth glanced around one last time, tucked her notes and writing utensil back into her reticule, and went to find Jane.

"No, no," said Fitzwilliam Darcy as he flipped the pages of yet another book in Hatchards' poetry section. "I am afraid this will not do."

"My apologies, sir," said the young attendant who had been attempting to help Darcy going on half an hour now. "But this is all the poetry in stock at present." He wrung his hands nervously. "'Twas just the Christmas season, sir. Books tend to make popular gifts, and we have not yet fully restocked our shelves."

Darcy looked up at the strain in the fellow's tone—it was clear the lad had grown weary from the unsuccessful endeavor—and slid the book he'd held back into its place. The poor soul appeared apprehensive of disappointing his customer, though Darcy had not issued any unkind words. He did sometimes have that effect on people, despite his intent for quite the opposite.

"It is no matter. I thank you for your help and require none further," Darcy said, and the clerk gave a small bow before apologizing once more and taking leave to assist another customer.

It wasn't the boy's fault anyway. Under normal circumstances, Darcy would have no trouble choosing a birthday gift for his younger sister; he had served as her guardian for years following their parents' early deaths and knew his beloved sibling well, but these last few months his mind had been elsewhere, and he had not

paid heed to current literature as attentively as was
his habit.

After leaving Netherfield, the country abode in
Hertfordshire leased to his good friend Charles Bingley,
Darcy's concentration was not as it should have been. Of
course, he maintained his responsibilities with care the
way he always had done, and his business acumen
remained intact, but he could not say the same for those
hours when he was not engaged in the management of his
properties. Moments of quiet leisure were the true cause
for concern, for it was during those moments that his focus
turned to a young woman he'd become acquainted with at
Netherfield and, for reasons still unknown to him, could
not quite release from his thoughts; it was almost as if his
own brain conspired against him.

His mind turned again, unbidden, to that same woman
now, and he decided to try a second time tomorrow to find
a present for Georgiana, perhaps at an earlier hour before
everything around him had a chance to remind him of Miss
Elizabeth Bennet. From the moment of their introduction,
the young woman had done all in her power to rile him,
and he had been convinced that leaving Bingley's country
home, and vowing never to return, would be all the
solution he would need to forget her.

Never in his life had he been so mistaken.

"Mr. Darcy, is that you, sir?" sung a soft voice from
behind.

He turned at the vaguely familiar sound to find Jane
Bennet standing before him, smiling pleasantly as
she bowed.

"Miss Bennet," he said, the greeting, as a result of his

surprise, coming out rather more gruffly than he would have liked as he bowed in return. "How do you do? I trust you and your family are well."

"Indeed, I am well, Mr. Darcy, and my family are in good health," Jane confirmed. "I hope the same is true of you and yours."

Darcy noted that she did not specifically include his friend in the wish, but he supposed he could hardly blame her, for he himself had discouraged Bingley's growing fondness for the lady. The eldest Miss Bennet appeared true to her word and indeed looked well, confirming Darcy's previous suspicion that she had not returned Bingley's interest with the fervor his friend had expressed —for if she had, surely she would not appear in such fine spirits now. In that, among other reasons, it seemed Darcy's disapproval of the match had been justified.

"Indeed, my family are all healthy and happy," Darcy answered.

Both were silent as a few seconds passed, Jane no doubt recalling the events of his time in Hertfordshire just as he was. Thankfully, they were surrounded by books, so there was no shortage of subjects to turn to before it was polite to bid their adieus.

"May I ask what brings you to Hatchards on such a cold day?" Darcy inquired.

Jane paused before answering, seeming to search for the right thing to say, and he wondered what disclosure she might be avoiding.

"We"—she hesitated—"that is to say, *I*…am simply browsing for something to read." Jane nodded as if to add finality to her less-than-sure statement.

"Would you not prefer to borrow from a lending library?" he asked. "I know of several here in London. I believe this very shop may offer a subscription."

He'd truly meant to be helpful, but the lady's complexion took on a brighter color and he understood instantly how callous he'd been to ask such a thing; it implied that the Bennets could not afford to purchase books to own, which he knew full well not to be the case, having heard much about the size and scope of their father's library.

"We are being careful of late, you see," Jane explained, all politeness despite his daft statement. "Our father had a spell not long after you and…your friends…departed from Netherfield, and it gave us all a scare." She paused. "In more than one way."

He should have apologized immediately for his indiscretion; he knew it as surely as he knew the names of his household staff, but somehow, he could not form the words. He believed himself so above Miss Bennet's station —had made that clear on more than one occasion when visiting her village—yet it was he who had made a terrible social blunder just now. Instead, he scolded himself silently and moved quickly to a sunnier topic.

"I am in search of a birthday gift for my sister, Georgiana," he explained, "and I am afraid I have not found the success for which I'd hoped."

"I am sorry to hear that," Jane said. "I am a lover of books myself," she added tentatively, clasping her hands together. "Do you suppose I might be of some help?"

She searched his eyes as he formed a response. She really was kind, Darcy thought, and her demeanor was such that he had never seen her anything but perfectly pleasant—very like his friend. It was no wonder that Bingley should have been attracted to her; unfortunately, attraction was of little importance regarding a proper marriage, and from what he had observed in his time at Netherfield, Jane possessed naught else where Bingley was concerned.

Still, he could not, and would not, behave toward her with less than gentlemanlike manners. He offered a smile.

"In what sort of books do you take particular interest?" he asked Jane.

She looked down at her hands. "Well, sir, I enjoy poetry, and the occasional novel." She paused. "But I am sure my sister is a more voracious reader than I, and would be far more advantageous to you in her recommendations."

At this, Jane's eyes, which had taken on a sudden look of excitement, shifted to a spot just over Darcy's shoulder, and his own curiosity, combined with an increased rate of breathing at the mention of the eldest Miss Bennet's sister, caused him to turn and look before he could think to do otherwise.

CHAPTER 2

If his breathing rate had increased before, now that very breath was stolen from him entirely as Miss Elizabeth Bennet approached. He had last seen her just over a fortnight ago, at Bingley's Netherfield ball, but he was quite certain her beauty had increased in that short time.

"Mr. Darcy," Elizabeth greeted, dipping into a bow.

"Miss Elizabeth," he replied, returning her gesture.

They exchanged pleasantries and then fell into a disconcerting silence which did nothing to quell the rapid beating of Darcy's heart.

The younger Miss Bennet's eyes sparkled with a teasing humor he had come to recognize as one of her defining characteristics, and curls spiraled away from the confines of her winter hat. She was bundled in warm clothing covered by a wool pelisse of forest green that accented her cheeks—a lovely color of pink, no doubt from the cold outside and the heat of the fireplace within.

The physical reality of her, standing before him as if

they had never parted, caused him to experience sensations he had spent the last month trying very hard to ignore.

"Miss Bennet informed me that you and your kin are well. Have you been long in Town?" he asked, hoping to learn the reason Elizabeth Bennet had come directly to the very place he'd sought to escape her.

"But a few weeks, sir," Elizabeth answered. "We have been visiting my uncle and aunt, Mr. and Mrs. Gardiner, in Cheapside. It is their custom to journey to Longbourn at Christmas, but my young cousin Edward injured his leg and cannot travel, so Jane and I came for the season while the rest of my family spent the holiday at home. We will remain another fortnight."

The mention of their temporary residence shamed him as he relived the unpleasant moments in which Bingley's sister, Caroline, had harshly ridiculed that part of London. It was but one of many of Caroline's comments to Elizabeth he wished he had the ability to expunge. A change of subject was in order.

"Your sister has just given a welcome offer of assistance," he explained, issuing what he hoped was a nice smile, and not that of a lunatic. He found it difficult to discern the difference in her presence, for she made him uncommonly nervous.

"Has she?" Elizabeth remarked, grinning at her elder sister with curiosity. "Of what sort, might I ask?"

"I was just telling Mr. Darcy that you may be able to suggest the perfect book as a gift for his sister's birthday," Jane answered, widening her eyes at Elizabeth as she stepped forward a little.

Something he could not interpret passed between the two women.

Darcy cleared his throat before speaking. "If I may be so bold as to inquire, Miss Elizabeth, have you read anything particularly fascinating of late, that you think a girl not too many years your junior might also enjoy?"

At this, Elizabeth smiled openly, which rendered her visage even prettier.

"Why should boldness give you pause, Mr. Darcy, when it has been my experience that you have not allowed it to do so before?"

There was a sharpness to her tone, and Darcy did not mistake its origin.

"Do you recall when last we spoke on the subject of books, Mr. Darcy, at the ball at Netherfield?" Elizabeth asked.

He nodded. "Indeed, I do."

On the occasion in question, Elizabeth had in no uncertain terms indicated that she and Darcy could not possibly be interested in similar reading material, or that if by chance they happened to be, the two were not likely to read those books with the same reaction.

"Then you are aware that you and I are unlikely to agree on what would constitute suitable reading for your sibling," Elizabeth said.

"On the contrary," Darcy argued. "It is precisely our perceived difference in taste that would qualify you to suggest a title, for you are bound to know more about what a young lady might want to read than I."

At this, Elizabeth blushed, and Darcy wondered if he had once again caused offense when his intention was in fact to show deference. Hoping not, he risked continuing. "I cannot know for certain, but I would wager you have read every title in your father's library at Longbourn, and one or two of them must have appealed to you."

He was rewarded with a reluctant but genuine smile.

"Very well," Elizabeth said. "I would warn against heavy history tomes. The lady would be quick to offer thanks for the gift in order to please the giver, and equally quick to later use the book as a doorstop."

Darcy could not help but chuckle at the jest, considering his penchant for favoring history books. "I imagine you are right," he conceded.

"Where hours of entertainment are sought rather than improvement of the mind—and, I confess, I find both of importance, in balance—I can whole-heartedly recommend the novels of Miss Fanny Burney, Miss Maria Edgeworth, or, if you do not object to a Gothic tone, Miss Ann Radcliffe."

He noted each author as Elizabeth spoke, none unfamiliar to him but none of whom he had read himself, and vowed to purchase volumes by all when next he braved the bookstore.

"I thank you very much for these suggestions, Miss Elizabeth," Darcy said. He looked down at her hands then, perhaps to avoid her pointed gaze, and noticed the top of a small notebook peeking out of her bag. He did not dare ask after its contents, but the eldest Miss Bennet must have detected his interest before he could hide it.

"My sister and I are here on special business," Jane said, and Elizabeth sent a look in her direction that would have induced Napoleon's surrender. But Jane, sturdier in will than the emperor himself, persisted. "We are collecting research for a book she is writing."

Jane seemed unable to stop herself despite the veritable daggers emanating from Elizabeth's eyes, but as for himself, Darcy could scarcely wait to hear more.

"It takes place partly in India and is a harrowing adventure. I, for one, cannot wait for my sister to compose more chapters," Jane said, only quieting when finally she dared glance over at Elizabeth.

He had witnessed many things in his eight and twenty years, but at this news, he could truly say he was all astonishment. Miss Elizabeth possessed the intelligence to pen a story—that much could not be denied—but the real question was why would a gentleman's daughter desire to do such a thing? This, of course, he would not ask her, but there was something else he could.

"And what is the subject of your study, Miss Elizabeth?" he inquired.

He found he could hardly await the answer, so deeply did he long to know, which defied logic and reason. The last time he had been in the presence of this woman, she had all but driven him mad with what seemed to be her great pleasure in vexing him. Apart from this, there was the matter of her family—a group of beings the likes of which Darcy had never encountered.

Mr. Bennet, though intelligent and witty, had struck Darcy as disinclined to consider the future wellbeing of his many daughters, and Mrs. Bennet, quite the opposite, so singularly bent on doing that very thing that she allowed all attempts at propriety to elude her. The youngest daughters, likewise, had not an ounce of decorum amongst them. All this resulted in Darcy's barely tolerating their company for a few hours, and he could not imagine having to do as much on a regular basis. His objection to the family in its entirety was so strong that he had unequivocally warned Bingley against any attachment to the eldest daughter, and he had not once doubted so doing. He strongly suspected none of the family's behavior had altered in the time since he and Bingley had taken leave of Netherfield.

So, what, then, could possibly account for the strange pull he felt toward Elizabeth Bennet now?

"It is nothing which would interest you, sir, of that I am sure," Elizabeth said in dismissal.

He would have to try another tactic, a bolder one this time, for he longed against all rationality to see her features return to a smile.

"If you require books for further research during your stay in Town—the library at Darcy House is not as extensive as the one at Pemberley, however you may find within it a volume or more which might suit your needs, as I am just given to understand your story takes place away from locations with which you are familiar," he said, alarming himself even as the offer spilled out. "You would come along too, of course," he added, addressing Jane before turning back to Elizabeth. "For propriety's sake, you need only say that you are calling on my sister, to whom I will be glad to introduce you as I believe you've much in common. At your beckon, I would send my carriage to keep you from walking in the cold."

Elizabeth appeared equally astonished at his

unexpected proposal, and her pretty rosebud mouth opened and closed but no words came forth.

Darcy indicated the portion of notebook in view at the top of her reticule. "Though it is a well-considered collection, I fear it would not impress a great reader such as yourself. Nevertheless, it may serve your needs as an authoress, so I offer it up to you all the same."

Mr. Darcy was rambling, which was so out of character for the man of few words she'd spent time with a month prior. Elizabeth looked at Jane—she of great betrayal who had revealed to an adversary their private reason for visiting the bookstore, a detail Elizabeth would address at a later time—and found her confusion reflected in her sister's expression.

Elizabeth wondered if Darcy was perhaps ill. What else could possibly explain his proposal that she use his personal library for her novel research? For one, it would not be proper for her to visit his home, as they were neither family nor old acquaintance, and they were not betrothed and had no such understanding. And for another, he did not even *like* her.

His capacity for causing her discomfort was unparalleled, though she would never allow him the satisfaction of possessing such insight, and she'd longed to quit the bookshop not moments hence he'd arrived in it.

"It is a kind offer, Mr. Darcy, and I thank you for your generosity," Elizabeth said, holding back the rest of her thoughts.

He seemed to be waiting for her to agree to his invitation; it would be polite to do so, despite the oddity of it, but it would also be a terrible idea. Sometimes it was best not to speak when one had too many things to say.

The gentleman nodded, and if she wasn't certain he was far too proud to experience such a sentiment, Elizabeth might have noted the hint of disappointment that passed quickly over his features before vanishing.

"Well, then. You both must have walked a very long way in the cold," Darcy said, his brow knit in such a way that, were he a different sort of man than she knew him to be from recent acquaintance, might have convinced Elizabeth of genuine concern.

"'It is not five kilometers, sir," she answered. "And Jane and I appreciate the invigoration of a walk out of doors."

"The snow is falling harder now," Darcy pressed on. "You must allow me to escort you home. My carriage is just out front and it is quite warm inside, I assure you."

When Elizabeth looked at her sister, Jane's eyes pleaded for her agreement.

"You are too kind, sir, but my uncle's footman is with us and we will enjoy the exertion," Elizabeth said, ignoring her desire to acquiesce, if only for a coal warmer underneath her feet.

Admittedly, it would be nice to receive transport back to Gracechurch Street in warm comfort, but she was sure she could not abide another minute with Mr. Darcy. She reminded herself silently of his prideful behavior when last they'd seen each other. And, though she had no proof of which to speak, she had convinced herself in the days hence that it was Darcy who had encouraged the parting of Bingley from Jane. There was no other way to account for Bingley's sudden withdrawal from Netherfield after the affection she'd witnessed between the amiable gentleman and her sister, and Elizabeth was all but certain Darcy had persuaded Bingley against the match; it would be just like him to do such a thing, so outwardly hostile had he been toward her family, so condemning of their station.

And even though she had to allow that the majority of the Bennets might have deserved the resentment, as far as Jane was concerned, Elizabeth could not forgive Darcy if he'd orchestrated the separation. Jane might conduct herself in company as though she were in good spirits, but Elizabeth could sense her sister's true inner feelings.

"I will not keep you from your enjoyment, then," Darcy said. "Good day, Miss Bennet." He bowed. "Miss Elizabeth."

"Good day, sir," the sisters replied, dipping their shoulders.

Though she had believed she would feel relief upon his exit, as Elizabeth watched Darcy stride toward the front door and away from her for the foreseeable future, something else struck her, something she would keep to herself until she took her last breath. For she could never, ever confess to anyone, not even her dearest companion and sister, that what filled her heart at his leaving…was regret.

CHAPTER 3

"Mr. Darcy seemed different somehow, Lizzy," Jane said through chattering teeth as the sisters walked in the direction of Gracechurch Street. They had marched most of the way in silence with James, a footman from Gardiner House, following a few paces behind, and had nearly reached their uncle's neighborhood; but the fierce wind made the remaining distance seem long.

Despite their linked arms and warm clothing, Elizabeth found her eyes moist and stinging and her hands nearly frozen inside kid gloves as they hurried past shops and houses with frosty windows.

Never mind, she thought; she was sure she had done the sensible thing in denying Darcy's offer of a carriage ride. For who was she if she would not stand by her principles, one of which was looking out for the wellbeing of her dear sister who was older but more charitable than she. A jolt of guilt in Elizabeth's stomach did not escape her as she considered the fact that journeying a considerable distance in frigid winter air did not exactly classify as *looking out for* Jane; it reminded her uncomfortably of a time when her mother had done something similar.

She consoled herself, however, by remembering that she and Jane had chosen to walk to and from the bookshop anyway. They were not the sort of women who stood around waiting idly for a knight in shining armor to rescue them, like Lydia and Kitty, and they were, after all, properly attired and chaperoned. She and Jane had survived much colder winter walks at home in Hertfordshire, where the wind was not buffeted by buildings as it was in London; they would not catch their death today.

"Lizzy," Jane prodded, her voice quiet around the hat Elizabeth had pulled down over her ears against the cold, "are you quite alright?"

"Oh, yes. Forgive me, dearest. I was lost in thought," Elizabeth answered.

When she looked over, Jane's brow was furrowed in concern.

"I just wondered if you found Mr. Darcy different from before, as I did," Jane continued. "He seemed very intent on your accepting his invitations, both to visit his library and to drive us back to our uncle's home. I am sure he was lighter of heart than he appeared to be at the Netherfield ball."

Elizabeth turned away to concentrate on putting one foot in front of the other. The snow fell faster and thicker, and it was becoming increasingly difficult to see more than a few yards ahead. There was activity yet on the pavement as shoppers hurried home with their purchases, but it had begun to wane along with the remaining daylight. At her side, Jane waited to hear her thoughts.

"I believe he only seems less prideful because he is in Town and must display the utmost in proper behavior, lest any of his peers witness his true nature," Elizabeth said carefully, though she was no longer certain she could determine with any great accuracy exactly what constituted his *true nature*.

Darcy had seemed to disdain her so upon their first meeting, when she'd overheard him saying that she was *not pretty enough to tempt him*, yet had shown interest in the workings of her mind and sought her opinion on a variety of subjects when she had gone to visit Jane, who had fallen ill following a perilous rain-soaked horse ride to Netherfield.

Then, on yet another occasion, when he'd stooped so low as to dance with her at a ball Bingley had given at his estate, Darcy had openly scorned the behavior displayed by her mother, younger sisters, and even her father. With his ever-changing estimation of her, how could she possibly know his mind when he seemed not to know it himself?

"Mr. Darcy is probably not so callous," said Jane. "I am sure that, given opportunity to display his finer qualities, he would surprise you. Have you considered that he may just not be comfortable showing his true feelings in the presence of new acquaintances? I am not so different myself. Perhaps if I had been more forthcoming about my fondness for Mr. Bingley…"

Jane's voice faltered and Elizabeth bit her lip.

"At any rate," Jane bravely continued, "you must admit he is exceedingly handsome. Beyond even what I recall when last we saw him. Of course, I would not have noticed as much at the time," she mused softly. "For my eye was drawn elsewhere, as my heart still is."

Elizabeth swallowed emotion that tickled the back of her throat at the reminder of Jane's fondness for Mr. Bingley. Then vexation rose up again, at the thought of Mr. Darcy's role in untying her sister from the person she truly loved. It did not help that Jane's assessment of Mr. Darcy was accurate—he was indeed handsome, though it pained Elizabeth to admit such a thing. His lithe, muscled frame, broad shoulders, and dark hair and eyes were impossible to overlook even with concerted effort.

"Well, we are not new acquaintances. I spent much time in his company during your stay at Netherfield, and many evenings passed during which his chief source of amusement was to challenge my every word. But yes, it is an unjust world in which one who fancies himself so superior to others should also be the beneficiary of dashing good looks," Elizabeth said, eliciting a grin from Jane. "And I would rather face a thousand wintery walks such as this one, in which I am overcome by cold that reaches deep into my bones, than to ever meet again the chill that follows that man wherever he goes."

"Then I am left to assume you are not likely to take him up on the offer of using his library?" Jane asked as they rounded a final corner and, blessedly, Gardiner House came into view.

"Not even if he were the sole possessor of a rare book I

needed for research," Elizabeth vowed with a huff. "Upon my word—I will never set foot in Mr. Darcy's library."

Oh, but it was nearly impossible to move forward in her writing when one vital piece of information was missing!

Elizabeth sighed heavily and set down her pen, longing for a break from struggling to complete the next scene of her novel. She really *must* find a way to fill in the details she needed in order to finish this chapter, which had plagued her all day.

The previous matter of geography had been sorted at the bookshop the day before, but shortly after she'd begun work the next morning, she had run straight into yet *another* tangle that would require an *additional* research book to unravel—one she had been unable to find in Hatchards. It was no wonder most women—indeed, most men—did not take up the practice of writing fiction; the effort not to lose one's very mind while so engaged required the sturdiest constitution.

"Pray, my dear niece, do tell Jane and me what irks you so!" called Aunt Gardiner from her seat near the hearth. "I wonder what correspondence could possibly cause such displeasure. I do hope nothing is amiss at Longbourn."

If only it were just a letter, Elizabeth thought but did not say as she covered her pages with a blank sheet of foolscap. Composing missives to her family and friends would have made a far simpler and, at present, more agreeable task.

"All is well, Aunt," Elizabeth said, gathering her work atop the writing desk to be dealt with another day, perhaps when her shallow well of patience had been refilled. "I am only tired."

"Come and join us by the fire, Lizzy, where it is warmer," Jane urged from the sofa. She grinned, a sparkle of mischief in her eye as Elizabeth drew near and sat in a chair across from her. "It is too dark in that corner to write *letters* at this hour anyway."

Elizabeth could not help but smile at her sister's teasing, which did much to lighten her mood. She sat back and studied her surroundings, soothed by the quiet peace and the company of two of her favorite companions. Uncle Gardiner had retired to his study after a cozy family dinner and Elizabeth's young cousins had long since gone to bed, leaving the ladies to themselves.

The Gardiners' drawing room was by no means large, but what it lacked in size it compensated for in comfort and simple elegance, with paneled walls and window dressings of a pale rose print against a backdrop of light green. Apart from the sitting area surrounding the hearth, there was a card table and chairs, glass-front bookcases of rich, dark wood filled with leather volumes, and the writing desk, tucked into a private corner, where Elizabeth had spent most of her mornings since she and Jane had arrived in London.

"You have it right, dear Jane," Elizabeth said. "I have done with writing, perhaps well past today." At this, she looked pointedly at her sister, whose features immediately registered disappointment.

But their secret was *their* secret—Mr. Darcy might

know of her novel's existence now, due to Jane's misguided insistence on helping with Elizabeth's research, coupled with her desire to discover the story's ending by any means necessary—but the sisters could not risk the news of Elizabeth's endeavor reaching any member of their family.

If their mother knew that her second daughter was attempting to earn funds by her pen rather than by an advantageous marriage, well...all the smelling salts in England could not save her.

Elizabeth shuddered at the thought.

"Lizzy," Aunt Gardiner began, setting down her sewing, "have you decided whether to accept Mr. Darcy's invitation to call and meet Miss Darcy?" Her expression gave away her eagerness to hear an answer.

Her mother's sister-in-law, Elizabeth was aware, thought very highly of the Darcy family because of their shared connection to Derbyshire, where Aunt Gardiner had spent time as a child. That she and her aunt could not agree on their impressions of Mr. Darcy was a matter of some contention.

Elizabeth glanced at Jane, who nodded her encouragement. They had chosen to reveal to their aunt only part of Darcy's invitation, relaying only that he wished to thank them for their help with his sister's birthday gift, and to allow them a chance to meet her. It was not necessary to mention the bit about his personal library, leading as it would to obvious questions.

"I have indeed decided," she answered, raising her shoulders a little in the hope of gaining bravery as she prepared to speak aloud the words she'd mulled over for the past hour, realizing as she had that she would have to put her manuscript's continuation on hold until a different solution could be reached.

Jane's eyebrows rose in surprise. "You have?" she echoed. "That is wonderful news!"

Oh, no. She has it all wrong, Elizabeth thought.

"You are very excited, Jane," their aunt exclaimed before Elizabeth could interject and set things straight.

"I am just happy to meet Miss Darcy," Jane said, her voice quite high-pitched. "Her brother cannot praise her enough, and it would be lovely to have a new acquaintance in Town. She is but a few years Lizzy's junior."

"You will be disappointed with my answer then," Elizabeth said, grimacing as Jane's smile collapsed, "as I am afraid I must refuse."

From their aunt, she omitted the truth that she had already done so regarding Darcy's offer to drive them home; on the matter of the use of his library, as she recalled, she had not been quite so firm, at least not in her verbal response. "We are acquainted from Netherfield, it is true, and it *is* kind of him to request a visit," she explained, not at all sure whether she fully agreed with her own statement.

Was it kind, really? Or did the man have some unspoken motive for asking them around? She could not yet draw any fixed conclusions about his character.

"But we are so very different, and Mr. Darcy does not even reside near Hertfordshire. I believe we would meet Miss Darcy only the once, and never see her again. It does not stand to reason that we should intrude on their family, if that is to be the case."

"You are not wrong on that account," Jane said, not meeting Elizabeth's eyes. "I suppose by your logic, it is for the best that we do not visit."

"I am sorry to hear that," Aunt Gardiner said, her tone solemn. "I know you have set your mind about Mr. Darcy, Lizzy. Yet, I still believe there must have been some kind of misunderstanding between you. For I cannot bear to think ill of someone from Derbyshire, and regarding his family, though we are not of the same circles, I have never heard a harsh word."

"A misunderstanding, indeed," Elizabeth scoffed.

Aunt Gardiner and Jane shared a glance that Elizabeth did not try to interpret.

"Well, a new year is nigh upon us and you will be here a few weeks yet, so anything could happen," her aunt said, smiling softly as she picked up her sewing. "In time, I believe all will be sorted. A person's true character cannot stay hidden for long."

CHAPTER 4

What kind of a damn fool... Darcy muttered to himself as his valet assisted him in dressing for breakfast. How could he have left two female acquaintances to walk such a long way home in the snow? His lack of action on the subject was simply abominable. He should have pressed harder... absolutely *insisted* that they ride in his carriage.

Oh, he was no gentleman today.

"Pardon, sir?" Roberts asked as he brushed a coat nearby.

Darcy cleared his throat, not realizing he'd been mumbling loud enough for his man to hear. "It is nothing that anyone can help me with, Roberts," he said. "Not even a man of your skill and experience."

Now, to Elizabeth Bennet's list of faults, Darcy could add: causing him to forfeit his manners, and to jabber to himself like a madman.

Roberts helped him on with his coat and left the room, and Darcy made his way downstairs to the morning room, where a delicious-looking spread awaited him on the sideboard. He had filled his plate with eggs and ham, and was in the middle of buttering a thick slice of toasted bread when a footman announced Bingley's arrival.

"Good morning!" Charles greeted cheerfully, entering the room. He accepted a plate from the footman and, as comfortable in Darcy's house as in his own, began to fill it before sitting at the table across from his friend.

"I was not expecting you until later, Charles," Darcy said before taking a sip of tea. He swallowed and placed the cup in its saucer. "Is everything alright?"

He studied his friend's face, noting brief hesitation before Charles gave an answer.

"All is well," Charles said, sounding, at least to his friend's ear, not entirely convinced at his own proclamation. He opened his mouth as if to say more, then decided against it.

"What is it?" Darcy prodded, folding his napkin on his lap.

Charles hadn't yet touched his food.

"Your features are not well suited to hiding things from an old friend," Darcy added with a grin.

Charles cleared his throat. "I have heard some news," he said, "from Caroline."

Darcy nodded, hoping his expression did not belie the unease he felt at hearing the name of Charles' sister. The lady had designs on him, he knew, and made no secret of her intention to convince him to marry her, an event which he swore on the souls of his beloved late parents, would never take place.

"It seems a pair of acquaintances from our time at

Netherfield have been here in Town these last weeks," Charles continued.

Suddenly, Darcy's breakfast did not sit well in his stomach. He did not say anything for a few moments, trying to decide whether to share the events of two days prior.

"Caroline has not visited them," Charles said. "Though upon hearing the news I encouraged her to do so. To my disappointment, she was not enthusiastic about the suggestion, but it would be improper for her to wait much longer, and I have no intention of offending connections who were nothing but kind to us during our stay in their village." He picked up his fork and began to poke at the eggs before him with excessive vigor.

The firmness with which his friend spoke did not escape Darcy, and made him keenly aware that Charles' feelings remained unchanged on the subject of Jane Bennet. He took a sip of tea and swallowed, buying time to think.

"I confess I have met them recently, while on an errand at Hatchards."

Charles dropped his fork and it crashed to the floor, prompting a footman to run over before he picked it up himself and wiped it on his napkin, thanking the servant as he waved the man away. "And you did not share this with me?" he asked, his expression dour. "Why ever not?"

"Charles…" Darcy began, pausing to gather his thoughts. His friend had a very different way of looking at the world than he, and, as strongly as Darcy believed it best to discourage the man's feelings for Miss Bennet, he did not wish to cause any more harm than necessary.

"I did not see the benefit in so doing. We were only briefly acquainted with the family. Miss Bennet and Miss Elizabeth are in London but a few more weeks and are occupied with their relations. I believe they were engaged for the Christmas season and will be leaving in but a fortnight."

Bingley's skin had turned a rather disconcerting shade of red. "So, I am given to understand you did not invite them to your upcoming ball, even though the whole of London will be attending?"

"Well, not the whole of it, surely. 'Tis only a private ball, after all, for a small number of—"

"The point eludes you," Charles interrupted through clenched teeth.

"As a matter of fact, it does not," Darcy explained. "The truth is, I gave an invitation of a different sort and was promptly rejected, therefore it did not stand to reason that I would issue another."

Charles narrowed his eyes. "I do not catch your meaning."

Overcome with sudden weariness—at Elizabeth's obvious dislike of him, at Charles' disapproval of the way he'd handled things, and at his own astonishment of how much it all mattered to him when indeed it should not—Darcy studied his friend closely.

"What I mean is, I am certain the Bennets want nothing more to do with me—with us," he said. "And I have chosen not to pursue the matter."

Charles' pale eyebrows rose so high on his forehead that they almost met with the edge of his curly blond hair.

"While I am not surprised to hear of this development, I cannot say I blame them."

He paused, running a hand over his face, ruddy with winter wind and frustration, then pointed a finger across the table at Darcy. "As your old friend, I will speak plainly; you have not behaved as your usual, honorable self where that family is concerned. I neglected to say so on prior occasions, which I regret, but it must be stated now."

"I had only your best interest in mind. I did not see your affection for Miss Bennet returned in equal measure, and I did not wish to see your heart broken by one particular lady when there are so many others who would be glad of your attention."

His countenance softening, Charles took a sip of tea before meeting his friend's gaze. "You may not have seen it, but I felt it. Perhaps with more time, I could have discerned with assurance whether her feelings were equal to mine. Unfortunately, as I now understand, the chance to do so is lost to me."

"Charles—"

Bingley held up a hand. "No, do not apologize."

"I was not going to," Darcy said. "At least not for my intentions. In suggesting we remove so quickly from Netherfield, I was only trying to save you from a marriage which, to be clear, I still maintain would not have resulted in your happiness."

"I will be the judge of that," Charles said firmly. "And you will make it possible for me to do so."

"By what means?" Darcy asked, though he'd begun to envision where this was leading.

Charles smiled broadly as he took a last sip of tea and picked up his fork, apparently intending to finally tuck into his breakfast. "You will invite them—the entire household —to your ball on the eve of the new year, of course."

Darcy sighed, but nodded in acquiescence. "That's what I was afraid you would say."

He had to admit there were certain truths included in his friend's little speech, and perhaps it would be for the best to let Charles grasp, once and for all, that Jane Bennet, though she'd shared a dance or two with him in Hertfordshire, did not return his love.

"It is settled then," Charles said, grinning as he banged a palm against the table, causing the footman to wince.

"I could not disagree more," Darcy countered. "Upon your request, I will invite the Gardiner household to the ball."

But in fact, nothing is settled, he thought.

And, he feared, where the profoundly exasperating Bennet sisters were concerned, it likely never would be.

If there was anything on Earth Elizabeth did not wish to receive two mornings later, it was another invitation from Mr. Darcy—this one tangible and composed in elegant masculine penmanship on superior quality paper. Nonetheless, that is exactly what transpired as she breakfasted with Jane and the Gardiners. And to think, she had just nearly succeeded in clearing him from her mind after their recent meeting; she could now only imagine that in another month's time she might have

forgotten the man entirely and been free to go on
with life.

She sighed heavily as her eyes wandered over the page,
inadvertently drawing the attention of her breakfast
companions.

Uncle Gardiner looked up from his eggs and ham and
offered his niece a hopeful smile from the head of the
table. Just behind him, a single ray of rare winter sunlight
peeked through a tall window that stretched along the
cheery morning room. "I do hope all is well, niece."

Elizabeth had the fleeting thought that on another day
—a day in which she had not seen or heard the name
Darcy—she might have better appreciated that cheeky
shard of sunlight and suggested a venture out into the park
to celebrate its presence.

This was not such a day.

She cleared her throat and arranged her features into a
pleasant expression that was quite the opposite of what she
felt. "It is, Uncle. All is as well as can be expected,
considering that it seems Jane and I will not be able to
evade Mr. Darcy any longer."

"Mr. Darcy?" Uncle Gardiner asked, turning then to his
wife who occupied the chair nearest his side. "Of your
Derbyshire, my dear?"

Aunt Gardiner looked to Elizabeth for clarification and
received a nod. "The very same. Of Pemberley," she
answered, dabbing quickly at her lips before placing the
napkin in her lap, freeing her hands to clasp together in
excitement.

Elizabeth found she envied her aunt; for she wished
she could muster the same reaction to having her presence

requested at such an event. "He has invited us to a ball at Darcy House on New Year's Eve," she explained. Unsurprisingly, this pronouncement was followed by glee all around the long breakfast table except, of course, at her own seat.

"Oh, it is kind of him to think of you both. You will have the most wonderful time," her aunt said, cheeks glowing almost as much as Elizabeth knew her own mother's would, had she made the same announcement at Longbourn.

Jane, who sat across from her sister, though slightly more subdued than the others, still lit up with energy. "We must have a look through the clothes we brought with us, Lizzy, and make certain we have proper gowns to wear."

"I imagine you are right, sister, though it will not just be you and I looking into our wardrobes," Elizabeth said, causing a brief ripple of quiet to descend upon the table before she explained her meaning. "We are all of us invited to the ball. You—Uncle and Aunt—as well, along with Jane and I."

"Well, dearest," Uncle Gardiner exclaimed to his wife, his eyebrows raised. "This is splendid news!" He looked at the three ladies. "We have been cooped up from the cold these last few days and an outing will do us a great deal of good, I believe." He turned again to their aunt. "I'd wager the ball begins late, so the children will not even have a chance to miss us."

The couple smiled warmly at one another.

As the rest continued in their eager anticipation of the upcoming party, Elizabeth, her appetite completely vanished, sank lower into her chair and asked herself, not for the first time since the morning at the bookshop, why on earth she had come to London at all.

And why, oh goodness why, despite all her effort, could she not seem to be rid of Mr. Darcy?

"Lizzy, can you really not agree that this is the perfect solution to your troubles?" Jane asked later that night, as the two readied for bed in their shared guest room.

"How can a ball at Darcy House be the perfect solution to anything?" Elizabeth countered as she pulled pins from her hair and began to run a brush through. "I cannot seem to escape the man," she said, not adding that her thoughts had indeed been fixated on him all day. "It was not enough to corner me in the bookstore; now he must have me captive in his own home so that he may vex me with utmost convenience."

She slammed the hairbrush down on the dressing table with far greater force than she had intended, causing Jane to wince. "I am beginning to think he was placed on this earth for the sole purpose of bringing about my distress."

Jane shook her head and stared at Elizabeth with incredulity. "It brings me no pleasure to realize I am right; indeed, you do not see." She slid a shift over her head, buttoned her bed jacket, and went to stand behind her sister, catching their reflection side-by-side in the mirror.

"Then by all means explain your reasoning to me," Elizabeth demanded. "For if you do not, I may very well lose what little patience remains in my possession."

Jane giggled and took up her sister's thick brown hair,

separating it into three sections before weaving them together. She had always been more accomplished when it came to plaiting and seemed to realize that Elizabeth would be soothed by the familiar ritual. "It is very simple, Lizzy. If you attend this ball, you will be inside Mr. Darcy's home."

It was Lizzy's turn to shake her head with lack of understanding.

"Where his library is!" Jane exclaimed. "Where his many books reside, waiting for just the right authoress to come along and explore their riches."

At this, Elizabeth began to grasp Jane's meaning. She peered into the mirror at her sibling, marveling for the countless time at how different the two were in both looks and personality. Yet Jane so thoroughly intuited the contents of her sister's heart.

Jane met her eyes and continued. "Though you will no doubt have a full card, I am sure you can invent a way to excuse yourself from dancing for a few moments by reason of a torn hem, the necessity of fresh air—anything, really—and wander off in search of his book room."

She finished braiding Elizabeth's hair and tied it neatly with a pale ribbon from the dresser top, then shrugged with utmost nonchalance. "There, you will locate the information your story is missing that has kept you from writing these last few days."

Elizabeth opened her mouth to speak but did not get a word out.

"Do not begin to tell me something has not been bothering you, because I know you, sister, and you are intolerably cross when you are not working on your book,"

Jane said, before continuing where she'd left off, ignoring Elizabeth, whose mouth still hung open in a most unladylike fashion. "After you locate what you require, you will return to dancing as if not a thing has happened—"

"And none shall be the wiser," Lizzy finished for her. "No dance partner would dare be so indecorous as to ask where I had got off to or with what feminine task I had been occupied."

She put a finger to her lips and then leapt from the chair. "My goodness, you are right, Jane. It is the perfect way to obtain the information I need for my manuscript, without accepting Mr. Darcy's invitation to use his library and in the process indebting myself to such a proud man."

"Precisely. As you saw at breakfast, our aunt and uncle would not imagine turning down such an invitation, despite its nearness to the event, and Aunt has insisted we accept so that she may send a response early in the morning."

Jane turned down the bedcovers and snuggled in, picking up a book from the bedside stand while she waited for Elizabeth to change into her night clothes. "Besides, Mama would never forgive Aunt if she allowed us to decline attendance to an event at which there are sure to be many eligible suitors."

"And, as the invitation includes all four of us, I will not be exclusively obliged to Mr. Darcy beyond our stay here at Gardiner House." Elizabeth donned her bed shift and jacket and got under the covers as Jane cracked open her book. "You know I could not abide such a thing. As soon as we leave for home, there will be no strings to attach us, and no further reason for Mr. Darcy ever to cross my path again. And most importantly, I can finally finish the scene that has been troubling me so and move on to the end of my story."

Elizabeth clapped her hands together. "Oh, it is perfect, Jane! Well done."

Perhaps, in addition to serving Elizabeth's research, attending a ball at Darcy House might give Jane a chance to renew her acquaintance with Mr. Bingley. For all her irritation where Mr. Darcy was concerned, Elizabeth did wish to resolve the matter of Bingley's sudden and unexplained withdrawal from Jane, if only to help her sister mend her heart in the interest of rediscovering hope. If anyone deserved happiness, it was dear Jane, and Lizzy would stop at nothing to ensure she had every chance to secure it for a lifetime.

Yes—even if that meant facing Mr. Darcy once again.

Quite content with this newly devised plan in place, Elizabeth snuggled beneath the warm covers and rested her head on the soft pillow, turning to stare out of the gauzy window covering at the night sky. She was too preoccupied with her own thoughts, which were focused on the plot of her novel and a list she had begun to devise of research tidbits she would collect as quickly as possible, once she'd found her way into the grand Darcy House library—to notice the satisfied smile that passed over Jane's lips, as she blew out the candle and bid her sister goodnight.

CHAPTER 5

"You appear exceedingly nervous, Darcy," Charles said by way of greeting as he entered the large drawing room of his friend's townhouse on the last night of the year. It had been transformed over the course of the morning into a most festive setting for a ball.

His staff had removed the furniture except for a few chairs placed here and there against the walls, and long mirrors were positioned about to extend the reach of light from the great chandelier above. Branches adorned the mantlepiece and tripods in each corner of the room, and seasonal floral arrangements had been selected as ornaments for the rest of the house, in areas through which guests would pass.

When Darcy chose not to respond—mostly because his friend's assessment of his inner feelings was not inaccurate —Charles continued.

"I realize that inviting them in the first instance hovered on the edge of propriety, as all the other invitations were delivered weeks ago. Yet, I maintain it was the right thing to do, for I must find Miss Bennet this evening and speak with her about…certain matters," he said, accepting, with a word of thanks, a glass of wassail from a passing footman.

At this, Darcy turned and spoke as firmly as he could while avoiding unwanted attention, considering his position as host. "Hovering on the edge of propriety? Really, Charles, I have gone so far over that edge of late, in the name of civility to the Bennet sisters, that I could not even see propriety should I turn back to look."

"Yes," Charles said, grinning as he raised the glass to his lips. "I wonder what might cause a man to behave in such a manner."

Darcy passed him a look that had on previous occasions struck dread in men who were not such close friends, but Bingley wasn't fazed.

As much as he loathed to admit it, Darcy was not wholly disappointed that the women of whom they spoke were soon likely to arrive. When last he'd seen her family in a setting such as this, many of the Bennets had behaved reprehensibly; how he wished such a scene might happen again. For all his efforts, he could not eradicate Elizabeth from his thoughts, and perhaps seeing her again might ease them if not altogether cease their constant interruption.

And no one would ever know what he himself would not even acknowledge: that, instead of leaving such business to her as he normally would, Darcy had spent hours with his housekeeper, selecting the finest, freshest bouquets of blossoms whose natural beauty he thought might please a certain someone, and that no expense had been spared. No one would know that he'd hired the very best musicians in all of London and bid them to play select songs he'd watched that certain someone dance to with merriment at the Netherfield ball.

It was sentimental nonsense, he very well knew, but for some reason it could not be stopped. He could thus only pray that fate might intervene on his behalf, to abolish the absurd feelings he'd begun to have for Miss Elizabeth Bennet.

"Oh, look," Charles said, handing off his barely drunk glass of wassail to Darcy. "There they are now."

As Darcy watched, astonished once again by his friend's complete lack of regard to hiding his feelings, Bingley brushed his hands down the front of his jacket and set off in the direction of...and there they were. As if his thoughts had turned into reality, Mr. and Mrs. Gardiner entered the ballroom, Miss Bennet and Miss Elizabeth directly behind.

Briskly, he forced himself to look away, turning to find his sister in conversation with Dowager Lady Godwin, a kind old woman of just the sort Georgiana preferred to befriend above others her own age—a characteristic for which he hoped he was not solely responsible.

After what had happened not so long ago between the dear girl and that most foul of men, George Wickham, he could not be certain. What he'd done, in chasing Wickham away from his sister, he could not regret—for the dishonorable man would have undoubtedly broken her heart in short succession. But he was aware that first romances—as he was certain Georgiana had imagined the short-lived match—could leave lasting marks. He hoped she would eventually find the courage to give her heart to someone else, someone deserving.

In the meantime, he was excessively relieved that Wickham had not set his sights on Elizabeth or any of her sisters while the regiment had been quartered in Meryton. The thought of that man going near another innocent was enough to make Darcy's blood boil.

No sooner had he downed the last of Bingley's wassail and handed off the empty glass than a footman arrived to introduce The Gardiners and the Bennets. Darcy bowed and the ladies curtseyed, and it was all he could do to remember to speak rather than stare openly as he would have liked, for Elizabeth Bennet was by far the most beautiful woman in the room.

She wore a red satin gown that highlighted the lovely glow of her cheeks, and her trim waist was accentuated by a band of gold about her bosom, an area from which he struggled to pull his gaze. Her dark, glossy hair was woven in a simple, elegant style with a matching band of gold tied round, and her deep brown eyes sparkled with flecks of light from the chandelier.

Darcy swallowed, willing years of practiced decorum to return from whence they'd disappeared so that he would not present himself as a complete and utter fool.

Mr. Gardiner issued a little cough. "We were so pleased to receive your invitation, Mr. Darcy. This winter has already proven fierce and will no doubt go on as it has begun. Your ball is a most welcome opportunity to escape the confines of our own drawing room."

Darcy found himself smiling at the man, whose

geniality was contagious, and about whom he had heard only kind words spoken from peers who knew him.

"Thank you, Mr. Gardiner. I am most glad you have all come." At this, he looked at Miss Elizabeth before he could stop himself and, if he wasn't mistaken, he'd caught a slight lift at the corner of her lips before she lowered her eyes.

"What a delightful ballroom, Mr. Darcy," Mrs. Gardiner complimented. "Very festive indeed. I must admit while I am always rather glum to see the Christmas season pass, I am looking forward to the coming year. I feel it will bring good things."

"I do hope you are right, Mrs. Gardiner," he answered. He did not know if she referred to anything specific, but he could not argue with such a warm wish.

Next, Miss Bennet offered equally kind greetings, as Darcy wondered fleetingly where Bingley had disappeared to, while Elizabeth, though polite, did not say more than necessary. And after a beat of quiet passed, Darcy turned to find his sister standing by his side, smiling up at him.

"Ah, Georgiana," he said. "I would like you to meet Mr. and Mrs. Gardiner, of Gracechurch Street, and Miss Bennet and Miss Elizabeth, their nieces, visiting from Hertfordshire."

As they began to speak to each other, Darcy noticed a friendship forming almost immediately between Elizabeth and his sister, and he wasn't sure whether to feel apprehensive or delighted. Hadn't he, only moments ago, felt a desire for her to have friends nearer her age? Elizabeth was only four or so years her senior and Georgiana often revealed herself to be an old soul, yet he knew he could not entirely encourage a bond between them until his own feelings had been sorted.

Before long, a footman arrived with another family of guests, and Darcy was forced to resume his duties as host, but he noticed that Elizabeth and Georgiana had not parted ways. After a few moments he could no longer see the two women amongst the guests, and a short while later, dancing had commenced.

Determined to find Elizabeth, Darcy began a turn about the room. He was obliged to dance with several ladies so as not to offend anyone at his own ball; nonetheless, he resolved to add his name to Elizabeth's dance card before it was full, an event that would no doubt take very little time as she was new to London and, without contest, the loveliest woman in the room. As he wandered, chatting here and there with his guests, he happened to glimpse Charles arm in arm with Miss Bennet, leading her into the next dance.

Despite his initial misgivings, he had to concede that there was a spark of light between the two, brighter even than the shimmering chandelier above, and there was a sudden vicelike grip on his heart as he realized he envied his old friend's obvious happiness in the company of another.

He wondered, not for the first time—would he ever find such contentment, such unmitigated joy, in the devotion of a woman? Or were happy wives and children reserved for men of different composition? Men such as Charles, who possessed a lightness of heart, joie de vivre, a gentler way of looking at the world and the people in it.

Perhaps Darcy himself was too guarded, too uneasy in

the company of others; perhaps he lacked the sort of carefree humor it would require to draw the attention of a loving partner. And that was exactly what he wanted, he knew full well—someone with whom to share the many peaks and valleys he had watched his own beloved parents weather over the years, always together, always united in their hopes and dreams, because of their enduring regard for one another.

Pushing these thoughts aside, Darcy visited with some of the people he had invited. Many were old friends of his parents, and their children, as the ball was a tradition of theirs he had continued after their deaths. As for his own friends, they were few but close, and the annual event was a chance to celebrate another year with those he cherished. After he was sure he'd spoken with all his guests, and all who wished to be were engaged in dancing, he decided he must find Elizabeth, though he had not an idea of what he might say once he succeeded.

All he knew for certain was that he felt drawn to her radiant energy in a way he could not control, for all his will to do so. It was as if invisible strings attached them, and an unseen hand had begun to tighten the strands, rendering it nigh impossible for him to pull away.

With Jane and Mr. Bingley occupied in dance for the next half hour, and her aunt and uncle engaged in conversation with another couple, Elizabeth glanced around to check that no one was watching her.

Confident that she was not the object of anyone's

interest, she ducked into the hallway and began her journey to the library. The string instruments, laughing voices, and clink of glasses that filled the ballroom drifted farther into the distance until they were drowned out by the sound of her own pulse pounding in her ears. Praying she would not cross paths with anyone in her acquaintance, Elizabeth hurried down the hallway and up a staircase adorned with winter greenery, the scent of it following her as she climbed toward the next floor, turning back ever so often to make sure she was not followed.

She tried to ignore the portraits of her host's ancestors as they gazed down at her from the walls, seeming to question the motivation for this clandestine errand.

If Mr. Darcy's townhouse, though far grander, was designed similarly to her uncle's, Elizabeth imagined she would find the library on this level.

She was not disappointed.

Tossing one last glance behind her, she opened the tall wooden door and slipped inside. Immediately closing it, she pressed her back against the door and shut her eyes as relief flooded in that she had not been caught. She would worry about the challenge of making it back to the ballroom later, she thought, pulling in a steadying breath.

At the moment, she had a more pressing objective and would allow nothing to stand in her way. She needed to sort out, with as much haste as possible, how Mr. Darcy organized his literature.

Elizabeth sought a certain document and had only blind hope on which to rely, for there was no guarantee at all that he would have it in his possession. As a place to begin, she thought of her father's book room at

Longbourn. Growing up, she had read almost every volume in Papa's collection, guided not by her father—who never once told her that she was not permitted to read any particular text, nor encouraged her to pick up any other—but by her own curiosity and interests. Though she could not say whether his method of letting her choose with such liberty was one she would wish repeated on her own children, Elizabeth was thankful for her own sake that she had been allowed that freedom. For she was certain she would not have become a writer—dare she call herself that?—if she had not been able to read so widely or so much.

Similarly, she had taught herself to compose stories by reading novels, pencil in hand and notepaper by her side as she deconstructed books she admired and studied the choices her favorite authors had made. Why this setting? This character trait? This plot? On top of which, she had a habit of watching and considering the behavior and speech of everyone in her company, for she did not think one could become a writer without first being a keen observer of human nature.

And *oh*, how she dreamed of being published!

It wasn't just that the income would help her mother and sisters, should any ill fate befall her father…no, no, it was more than that.

If she could earn enough as a novelist, even if no one knew the work was her own, she would have the option of denouncing marriage and all its trappings, for she could think of nothing so great as the freedom to live as she pleased—to spend her days reading and working rather than simply existing as someone's wife. She could not imagine a scenario in which marriage would bring more satisfaction than that of remaining single and self-reliant.

Well...perhaps that was not *entirely* true.

Even without seeing it for herself, she may have imagined a time or two what it might be like to be mistress of Pemberley.

If her aunt's stories about the Darcy family seat were not exaggerated, it must be very grand indeed. But such a thing would require becoming Mr. Darcy's wife, and to be permanently attached to such a judgmental, ill-humored, dour man...well...it would be an unthinkable burden, best left to some other poor soul.

She searched the library, wandering quietly through shelves that reached nearly all the way up to the high ceiling. Contrary to its owner, the room had a warm, inviting feel, and Elizabeth imagined curling up in one of the many plush armchairs near the softly glowing fireplace, with a book and a cup of tea.

Alas, there was no time to indulge in fantasy, and after several moments, she finally found what she was looking for in a large bound volume: papers, from exactly the year she required, presented to the House of Commons from the East India Company.

After lifting down the heavy book, she began to thumb through the pages, taking great care not to leave behind any creases.

And there it was, at last! The exact detail she needed to add accuracy and real-life resonance to Thomas and Meera's next scene together in her story.

Instead of bringing along the weightier notebook this time, Elizabeth had simply tucked into her bag the pertinent manuscript pages, folded into quarters, so that she could add in the information directly. Setting the open book down briefly on a small end table, she pulled out her papers and spread them inside the volume while she made her additions with a pencil stub; then she picked all of it back up and was about to replace the book when...

"You seem to have a keen interest in that volume, especially as someone who adamantly warned against gifting my sister with history books."

Elizabeth let out a yelp as she slammed the book closed and it slid from her hands, landing on the floor with a loud crash.

"What on earth!" she shouted, spinning abruptly to find Mr. Darcy staring at her with his arms crossed— smiling, no less, like a Cheshire cat.

CHAPTER 6

"I apologize for startling you, Miss Elizabeth," he said, trying with little success to adjust his features into a more serious expression.

"I daresay your vain attempts to stifle your laughter make it rather impossible to believe a word of that statement, Mr. Darcy," she countered as he bent to pick up the book.

He handed it gently over to her rather than returning it to the shelf himself. Another person might have paid no care to the gesture, but to her it indicated that she wasn't entirely unwelcome, and that she might be permitted to continue perusing the volume if she so wished.

Mr. Darcy gazed at her a long moment before speaking, and all she could think to do was to grip the book tightly while holding her chin up high, ready to accept whatever admonishment he was well within his rights to deliver. She was painfully aware that she had no business trespassing this far into his home, and had rather vehemently neglected all attention to propriety; alongside which, she was not equipped with an excuse for her behavior that any reasonable person could be expected to understand.

"The reason for my amusement is that I did not expect to discover you here, and I am quite surprised," he said, offering an elbow as he drew the other arm behind his back. "If you would like, Miss Elizabeth, I am happy to escort you back downstairs so that you may return to the festivities. I am sure you will be missed before much time has passed."

She did not accept his offer. "You are quite right, Mr. Darcy. However, I do not see how we will make it back to the ballroom without being noticed, and I do not wish to encourage any curious gossipers to invent a fictional reason as to why I might have wandered up the stairs of this lovely home."

Had she seen what she thought she saw? If she was not mistaken, the stoic, hard-hearted Darcy's eyes had widened ever so briefly at her blunt statement, before returning to their usual penetrating stare.

"Then what do you propose we do, Miss Elizabeth? For the same reason you mentioned, we cannot very well stay here in the library indefinitely." He held out a palm as though to emphasize his point.

Pulling her eyes away from his, she looked around the room and found no solution to their predicament.

Seconds continued to pass as she remained mute. To make matters worse, her cheeks began to warm—from the fire, or from her host's justified but unwelcome intrusion on her errand, she could not discern—and she longed for a drink of something cool to soothe the increasing dryness of her mouth.

He moved forward a single step. "Are you quite alright?" he asked, reaching out a hand. "I must say, you look suddenly unwell."

She passed him the book and he set it aside, after which she did accept the elbow he once again offered and allowed him to lead her to a large window. It was impossible not to take notice of their proximity, and the sudden nearness of his masculine energy did nothing to calm her already frayed nerves.

"It is cooler here," he said, studying her face. "Rest a moment."

Not accustomed to being looked after in this way by a man, Elizabeth stood motionless at first but then did as he suggested, and he occupied the seat across from her.

"In the interest of easing your mind, I should inform you that there was no one in the hall when I came in, and I take care to employ only staff who uphold a certain level of discretion. Not that I have anything to conceal," he added quickly. "Just that I have always required that the people in my household respect my family's privacy, as any prudent master would."

He paused. "When you are ready to return to the party, I will ensure that you are able to do so without unwanted attention."

Elizabeth nodded at his words but could not relax into the chair for all its plush comfort; she sat stiffly with her reticule in her lap. Mr. Darcy's comment about his staff's discretion could easily be construed as a reprimand to her, for she had certainly invaded his privacy by coming into his library without invitation and, whether he had intended it, she felt properly chastised, as well she should.

"It is my turn to apologize, Mr. Darcy, for wandering this far into your house and for making use of your library without permission. I may appear stubborn and impetuous —as my mother has brought to my awareness on more than one occasion—but I will admit when I am wrong."

Oh, but it was so difficult to do so, especially to such a man, who owed profuse apology to her sister—rather, her entire family.

His expression was indecipherable.

"You are mistaken, Miss Elizabeth. As you will recall, I did in fact welcome you to use my library. I just did not imagine you would go about it in quite this manner." He raised an eyebrow. "Miss Elizabeth, does this…quest… have anything to do with the book that your sister revealed you are writing, upon our recent encounter at Hatchards?"

Elizabeth issued a little puff of breath and fidgeted with her beaded bag, not meeting his eyes. "*Revealed* is certainly an apt choice of word. I did not intend for anyone to know of my project until I am ready to publish someday —if doing so does not turn out to be far too ambitious a design."

At this, Mr. Darcy's features softened and Elizabeth caught sight of a little tick of motion at the intersection where his sculpted jaw met the softer shell of his ear, triggering a similar jump of her own heartbeat. Though he did not smile, she had a clear sense that he was not angry with her for her actions that evening, and this caused more uneasiness than if, perhaps, he had shouted and demanded she leave the room at once.

She was accustomed to the stern, unfeeling Mr. Darcy whose company she had endured at Netherfield; this version of him was different, and she found the change perplexing. All the while, a ball carried on downstairs and guests would surely soon begin to wonder what had become of their host.

"Why should publishing your work be too ambitious?" he asked, the tone of his voice indicating that he genuinely longed to know her answer.

He leaned forward slightly. "You are intelligent and perhaps more well-read than most in my acquaintance. Certainly, if anyone has the ability and determination to write a novel that others want to read, it is yourself."

Elizabeth's pulse sped up to an alarming rate and her breath caught in her throat. What on earth had enticed Mr. Darcy to pay her such a compliment? And more importantly, why did it affect her so?

"Indeed, I see no reason why you should not be published many times over, if that is the direction in which you endeavor," he added.

She swallowed and forced herself to speak, though the words dispensed were shaky and less self-assured than her ordinary voice. "Thank you. That is kind of you to say."

He gazed at her with disquieting warmth and Elizabeth noticed, not for the first time, how very dark were his eyes, their mahogany depths intense and startling.

She wondered what he experienced when he looked at her. Was it the same irritation and exasperation he'd seemed to feel so strongly when first they'd met, and many times thereafter until his departure from Hertfordshire…or was it something milder now?

"Whatever our differences, Miss Elizabeth—the multitude of which you did not hesitate to impress upon me as your sister recovered from her illness at Netherfield —they cannot be the sole reason for your intense dislike of me."

He moved forward in his chair until his knees were mere inches away from touching hers, and Elizabeth sensed that if such an event were to occur, she would feel the electricity of that contact all the way up into her chest.

She had never before been alone in a room with a man who was not a member of her family—should not have been even then—but despite all rationality, she recognized that she could trust Mr. Darcy to be a true gentleman in any circumstance. For that reason, she did not jump from her seat and run for the library door; rather, she relaxed back into it and considered his account.

"On the contrary, Mr. Darcy. It is you who made no secret of your abhorrence of me—indeed, of my entire family," she said, gripping tightly the gold ribbons that adorned her reticule. "And though I am without evidence, I strongly suspect that you are at least in part responsible for the sudden departure of Mr. Bingley from Netherfield, an occurrence which caused in my dear sister the severest wound I have ever known her to suffer."

He folded his hands and looked downward into his lap to study them as the fire crackled, and several seconds ticked by on a majestic grandfather clock in a far corner of the library.

The irony of feeling so ill at ease in a room that was obviously meant to invoke calm and comfort did not escape Elizabeth's awareness. She concentrated on breathing slowly in the hope of steadying the rapid beat of her heart.

Up until that very moment, she had only been willing to give credence to her anger and frustration where Mr. Darcy was concerned. Now—piercingly aware of its presence—she acknowledged the hurt that hid beneath.

"Your accusation is not without merit," he said, finally breaking the thick silence. "If you can spare another few moments here with me, I would be grateful for a chance to explain my actions."

She met his eyes and found within no sign that she should doubt his sincerity. Not possessed of an appropriate response and, as well, quite curious about what he might reveal regarding his previous behavior, Elizabeth simply nodded and offered her full attention.

"I confess that, upon spending time in the company of your mother, father, and three younger sisters, I was often astonished at their want of propriety," he began, pressing his long fingers together. "And, having witnessed as much, I determined that a marriage between one of my most treasured friends and your eldest sister—inasmuch as it would forever bond him to such a family—would not be acceptable."

Elizabeth shifted in her seat. Mr. Darcy's brows knit, and several conflicting emotions seemed at war behind his dark eyes.

"I have not the same grievance against Miss Bennet and yourself, if that holds any merit in your opinion."

"If you had even a little concern for my opinion, Mr. Darcy," Elizabeth said, her voice unsteady, "I venture you would not have taken such hasty action—the result of which has caused my sister unspeakable sorrow—without first seeking consultation with your friend."

She raised her chin and stared at him as though they were on opposite sides of a battlefield. "You may have Mr. Bingley's best interest in mind, or so believe you do, but you are not his keeper, and in my opinion, you are not at liberty to make decisions for him about what lies within his heart."

Looking not a little contrite, he reached out a hand and opened his mouth to speak, then let his palm fall back against his knee without a word.

Elizabeth's anxious heart fluttered inside her chest and threatened to burst free and fly straight out of the window. She was still angry, yes, but she was also grateful for the chance to air out the frustrations she had been carrying around these past weeks.

"I must admit that I did alert my friend to the inevitable peril of such a match," he said quietly.

At this, Elizabeth stiffened, but held her tongue. Aware since childhood of her tendency toward drawing swift conclusions, she knew it was only fair to let the man finish explaining his conduct before she sentenced him, at least within her heart, to complete condemnation.

Mr. Darcy went on. "But it was not only the unsuitable nature of Mr. Bingley's and Miss Bennet's possible courtship that turned me against the idea. There was also the matter of Miss Bennet herself."

"What can you mean?" Elizabeth interrupted, unable to maintain patience despite her promise to herself to hear him out. To receive criticism of her younger siblings and parents was one matter; she would not tolerate the same directed toward Jane.

"As genial and impressionable as my friend is wont to be, I do not at all believe that I have it in my power to have set him against Miss Bennet on my own. It was your sister's lack of interest in him that permitted me to determine with confidence that the two of them should not be encouraged any further. I—"

Elizabeth held up a hand. "Mr. Darcy, with all due respect, I must stop you from saying any more on the subject of my sister. For you have wildly misjudged the contents of her heart, and I cannot permit you to continue without correction."

She stopped speaking and pulled in a long breath of air, praying for patience and calm in the face of his outrageous remarks.

When she dared look up again, Elizabeth saw that Mr. Darcy had not taken her rebuke lightly.

CHAPTER 7

"I know what I saw," Darcy argued with more force than he intended. How was it that Elizabeth had the power to rile him so and cause him to question everything he'd done, even when he was absolutely certain it had all been in the best interest of those he cared for?

"Miss Bennet did seem delighted to receive the attentions of Mr. Bingley," he continued, "but no more, I observed, than those of any others with whom she shared dances, and thus I deduced that she reserved no unique fondness for my friend."

"You know what you *think* you saw," Elizabeth said, moving to the edge of her seat. "But I am afraid you judged inaccurately."

Closing her eyes, she pressed her thumb and forefinger around the bridge of her nose and Darcy felt a pang of remorse for having caused such distress in a woman he...

He *what* exactly?

When he had left the ballroom in search of the lady, he

had been drawn to the library by an unseen force, as if his body knew instinctively where she would be found.

Not a sliver of consideration had he given to what guests might think when they noticed his absence, or what he would do if he was successful in locating her; he'd simply followed the pull, as the tide obeys the moon. And when he'd opened the library doors to catch sight of her standing in a far corner—slender shoulders hunched over, nose deep in a heavy tome as she scribbled something on a piece of paper—the lure had grown stronger still.

The tension had not alleviated until he had offered the crook of his elbow and she'd taken it, the innocent embrace sending a pleasant shiver along his spine...as though having her there, tucked safely against him, was the most natural thing in the world.

Yet, that could not possibly be right...could it? He was certain Elizabeth loathed the very mention of his name.

At that moment, she only peered at him with obvious disappointment, and he found he very much wanted to make things right, to change her mind about him so that she might regard him in a better light.

"You see, Mr. Darcy," she said, laying her gloved palms open atop her lap. "My sisters and I have spent much of our lives at home rather than in the society of others—especially suitors."

She paused, appearing to carefully measure her next words. "I suppose we have not been given chance enough to learn what should and should not be revealed when it comes to matters of the heart, and Jane was guarding hers carefully. She wanted more than anything to believe that Mr. Bingley returned her affection—and I can assure you of its sincerity—but I imagine she did not know the proper way to ask, having never before experienced anything akin to his admiration. My family, none more than Jane, were all surprised when he danced twice with her at the Netherfield ball only to depart without so much as a friendly goodbye. I now know with certainty what I believed all along to be true—that you, Mr. Darcy, were the catalyst in his decision to leave."

Darcy was quite sure he had never felt more deplorable than he did at that very moment. His heart pounded in his chest with great ferocity as he resolved to speak plainly without first censoring his thoughts.

He took a deep breath. "I cannot deny your charge, Miss Elizabeth, and it appears I have been remiss in judging you and your eldest sister much too severely. I understand, having had the pleasure of knowing you a little better from our time together during Miss Bennet's illness at Netherfield, from meeting you again at Hatchards, and talking with you here now, that you are entirely your own creature, singular of mind and spirit, quite without comparison. In addition to realizing my error, I daresay I find myself wanting to spend more time in your company, and wanting to hear your opinion on all things, despite knowing you are determined to have it differ from mine."

At this last admission, he could not stop himself from grinning. He was teasing her, and he hoped she would grasp the tenderness behind his words.

He was rewarded mightily when her lips turned up at the corners and her eyes met his.

"I am grateful for your apology on this count, Mr. Darcy." The hard-won smile faded as quickly as it had come. "However, you are not admitted into my good opinion just yet."

He held out his hands. "Allow me to add that it was never my intention to cause your sister pain. Had I known the depth of her fondness for my friend, I might have been more inclined to weigh that over the conduct I witnessed of your family. For I would not endeavor to deny Mr. Bingley true happiness."

The lady did not speak, as she appeared to consider what he now viewed as his great transgression.

He was truly sorry for having interfered in Bingley's pursuit of Miss Bennet, and in light of the information he now possessed, he had no reason not to take confidence in Elizabeth's explanation; for her superior knowledge of her sister must make her account truthful.

She took a deep breath and closed her eyes briefly before opening them again. "It pains me to acknowledge it, but you are not altogether wrong in your assessment of my parents and younger siblings."

As much as he would have thought otherwise, he was not the least bit pleased to be in the right, under such circumstance.

Elizabeth continued. "I have been aware for quite some time that my father's lack of guidance and propriety may well be cause for my sisters' poor chances of securing comfortable futures. As a grown woman, I've come to understand that my parents were themselves ill-matched, and over time, they have turned toward their own separate endeavors. My father prefers his books and the country above society, and my mother is not equipped to make up for his lack of attention to the well-being of my siblings."

The note of sad resignation in her voice was enough to break Darcy's heart.

"I am all astonishment at receiving your apology, but it is most welcome," she said, the seriousness in her eyes pinning him to the chair. "You have absolved yourself of guilt where my sister is concerned, but I must insist that you address the issue with Mr. Bingley, and see to it that he is made aware of Jane's regard for him before it is too late."

Darcy nodded enthusiastically. "I will do so with haste," he promised. "Miss Bennet"—he paused, carefully measuring his next words—"It must have been arduous for you to reveal to me that your upbringing was not all it should have been. You and your sisters ought to have been given every opportunity to find security and happiness. Yet, no family is perfect, and you have become a delightful person in your own right. In spending time with you, my respect and admiration for you has increased mightily. You are right to have judged me harshly for my actions. I can only hope that, in time, you might be able to forgive me for the distress I have caused your sister, as well as—I now understand—yourself."

Elizabeth nodded, and Darcy was overcome with liberation at having shared the burdens that had for so long occupied his mind. As well, his fondness for Elizabeth only increased each time they were in company together, so much so that he now longed to share something else with her…

His heart.

It seemed such a simple thing. After all, he had learned that she embodied everything he could possibly desire in a wife: intelligence, wit, loyalty, and even beauty, which, while not vital to sustaining an excellent partnership, was certainly pleasing.

Yes, it *seemed* a simple thing, but Elizabeth Bennet deserved the very best he had to offer. Somehow, he knew that finding the right way to convey his burgeoning affection for her would be anything but simple, though that is exactly what he resolved to do.

Darcy stood up from his chair and reached out a hand to assist Elizabeth from hers.

"Though it displeases me that our time together must draw to a close, I am afraid I must return you to the ball, Miss Bennet. We do not want you declared missing and a search party sent out."

She smiled as she accepted his hand, her eyes sparkling with the same warmth that surged inside his own chest, and never before had he felt such dire hatred of women's gloves for the barrier they produced between her skin and his own.

"I am glad to know that you no longer despise the very sight of me, Miss Bennet," he said, guiding her toward the library doors.

"As am I, Mr. Darcy. For it has been a long, harsh winter already, and I do not wish to hold onto the chill any longer than necessary."

He paused just in front of the fireplace, to relish one last look at her glowing loveliness before he would be forced to share her presence with his guests.

"The winter has been long, perhaps," he replied, meeting her gaze. "But not so harsh—I am sure—given present company."

Though she could hardly think of eating when such unexpected events had transpired, it was soon time for supper. Mr. Darcy, having assisted Elizabeth in discreetly exiting the library and returning to the ballroom as promised, followed only after she had re-entered and enlightened Aunt Gardiner to a mythical tear in the hem of her gown as the cause for her lengthy absence, while subtly passing a glance to Jane that only her sister would understand.

After this exchange with her family members, Mr. Darcy had approached their group and, without a single hint that he'd just spent nearly half an hour talking with her privately, asked Elizabeth if she cared to dance. Of course, having neglected to fill her card as a result of her prolonged disappearance from the ballroom, meanwhile engaged in conversation with that very man, she could scarcely answer in any way except the positive, and he whisked her off on his arm.

Much to her wonder, the next half hour was one of the most pleasurable of Elizabeth's life, and she found when the music ceased that she longed for endless more moments in his arms.

So much had changed in so little time. With the matter of Jane and Mr. Bingley's parting resolved, there was naught else to stand in her way of sketching Mr. Darcy's true character...

And she had begun to like what she saw.

As the clock struck midnight just before the meal, guests gathered round to sing "Auld Lang Syne" to ring in the new year, and Mr. Darcy surprised Elizabeth once again that evening by asking her to accompany the vocals, as he stood by to turn the pages of her music.

Ordinarily, she would have refused and insisted that someone with sharper talent play the tune, but how could she do so then? He asked with such obvious enthusiasm alighting his features, and the gesture—in front of his guests at a grand private ball—honored her and warmed her spirit in such a way that she acquiesced almost immediately.

Elizabeth was so delighted at this occurrence, in fact, that she did not even take any particular joy when, out of the corner of her eye, she saw Caroline Bingley's face twist up as though the lady had swallowed a lemon.

After the party had sung the last verse—with far more vigor than actual talent—Mr. Darcy offered Elizabeth his arm and led her into the dining room, where he helped her into the seat next to his. The evening progressed in much the same way, Elizabeth relishing the unexpected but nonetheless lovely consideration from someone for whom, only hours ago, she could not have spared a kind word.

Though Elizabeth was not the only one who noticed his devotion to her; for Miss Bingley declared loudly enough so that the whole of the long table was privy, that Elizabeth had "quite commandeered the attention of their host that evening," and asked that she "kindly try sharing a little."

To which Mr. Darcy—his gaze fixed upon Elizabeth so that she felt truly the most beautiful woman in the world—replied that, indeed, he was the captain of his own mind and would not allow it to be steered in a direction he did not wish to travel.

And by the time they'd finished the white soup, cold meats, vegetables, and cakes, Elizabeth was certain the flush in her cheeks and the lightness of her heart were all due to Mr. Darcy, and not the very fine claret.

CHAPTER 8

A few hours later, as they rode in Uncle Gardiner's carriage back to Gracechurch Street, Jane was in such high spirits that she could not confine her energy to the space of her own body, and thus grasped Elizabeth's hand so tightly that Elizabeth was sure she would have a cramp when she tried to write the next morning.

"Jane," she admonished lightly, "do have a care for my poor bones."

"I am dreadfully sorry," her sister whispered, trying not to draw attention from their aunt and uncle. "It is just that I cannot contain my excitement."

Elizabeth's heart swelled at Jane's wide, contented smile, a sight she had not borne the pleasure of in far too long. "Do you think he will propose?" she asked, unable to help herself.

At this, Aunt Gardiner's ears perked up and she ceased chatting with her husband to stare at her nieces on the bench across from her.

"Did I hear the word I think I heard?" she asked.
"Please whisper a bit louder," their aunt added, laughing.
"For your uncle and I could do with a diversion from
this cold."

Though a footwarmer rested beneath the ladies'
slippered feet, and all were draped in fur blankets, the
night air was frigid indeed. Thankfully, the journey back to
Gardiner House was not too far a distance.

Jane, eyes wide, cast a glance toward Elizabeth, who
spoke for her shy sister.

"We were simply remarking on the attention paid
Jane by a certain gentleman we enjoyed the happy
occasion of meeting at Netherfield," she explained,
knowing full well her aunt would push for more, and not
at all displeased by the knowledge. Elizabeth was only
too glad to share Jane's renewed joy, buoyed by the
insight that—this time—there would be nothing to stand
in the way of true love.

Aunt Gardiner's gloved hands clasped together at her
chin. "Are we talking of Mr. Bingley?" she asked, hopeful.

"Indeed, we are," Elizabeth said, grinning as Jane's
already pink cheeks blushed an even rosier shade.

"Oh, how delightful!" their aunt exclaimed. "I know
your mother would very much love to see you settled,
sweet Jane, and I speak for us all when I say we would be
thrilled to see you in a happy marriage."

She glanced at her husband with soft, adoring eyes.
"For such a match has been a lifelong blessing for your
uncle and me, has it not, dear?"

Uncle Gardiner returned his wife's gaze. "Indeed, it
has," he said, adding, "I am convinced there is no greater

treasure in life than a joyful marriage and the children it brings."

"I hasten to add," Jane said, "that Mr. Bingley has not yet asked for my hand." Her eyes glimmered with obvious fondness for the subject of their conversation. "He only danced with me many times and assured me of his enduring affection."

She gave them all stern glances…well…as stern as they could be, coming as they did from such a kindhearted person.

"It is only a matter of time," Elizabeth interjected. And now it was her turn to squeeze Jane's hand.

"I hope you are right," Jane said.

To which Elizabeth responded cheekily, "Am I ever wrong?"

Later that night, Darcy tossed and turned in his bed until the sheets had become such a jumble that he was forced out in order to set them right, at which point he concluded that there was no point continuing unsuccessfully to try and capture the sleep that eluded him.

He was well and truly exhausted after planning and hosting a ball, in addition to the remarkable events that had unfolded between him and Elizabeth.

So, what was it that vexed him and would not allow a moment's rest?

The fire in his bedroom had died down to only a few glowing embers and the room was cold, so Darcy donned his robe and paced from his bed to the hearth and back again, until at long last, a memory surfaced.

Walking back through the events in his mind, he recalled that Elizabeth had been writing something with a pencil in the book she had dropped when he surprised her in the library.

Yes, that was it. He had picked up the large volume and handed it back to her and she had accepted it. Then, she returned it back to him and he'd set it down somewhere, perhaps on a side table; but, if memory served, she had not ever retrieved her notes from the book.

Darcy walked over to the window and looked out at the street below, allowing himself to fixate on that little bit of information for just a second, flattering himself that her reason for distraction was the conversation that had followed.

Was it possible she had been as engrossed in his company as he had been in the pleasure of hers? The very thought caused his lips to turn up at one corner, and only a moment later he had left the master suite for the library.

Candle in hand, he opened the doors and stepped into cool darkness, waving the light gently about until his eyes rested on the book he sought, and a question pressed on him with increasing fervor—what had she written and abandoned there between the pages?

Even as he treaded quietly across the carpet toward the answer, Darcy knew he shouldn't look.

Whatever notes the lady had composed belonged to her, no matter that she'd left them behind in his own library. What he should do—his conscience prodded with vigor—was to recover Elizabeth's papers from his book and return them to her. And that is exactly what he planned to do…after he had a brief glance.

He knew she was writing a novel that surely one day she would wish to publish. Whatever she had written would not be anything like a private diary. Was it any wonder that he longed to know everything that could be known about Elizabeth?

While he'd been talking with her earlier, an idea had begun to form about a way in which he could help her. He knew a publisher in the city—an old friend of his father's, whose own son was Darcy's mate from university. Billings' growing house published primarily novels and poetry, and his company had an excellent reputation for presenting literature of the highest quality, always in the most beautiful bindings.

The more he thought about it, the more it seemed the perfect plan.

He would be helping Miss Elizabeth realize a dream.

He had seen when her sister had spoken of her writing, how much it mattered to her, and he knew without having looked yet himself that her writing, like her intelligence and wit, would make for delightful reading. He had only to speak to Billings and set his plan into motion.

It also did not escape Darcy's understanding that, perhaps, if Elizabeth was pleased with what he hoped would be an offer from Billings to publish her novel…she might begin to see Darcy for what he was: a man falling deeper and deeper in love with her each moment he spent in her company.

Surely, *surely*, if he succeeded in securing the promise of a publishing contract for her, she might begin to reconsider her initial impression of him; their time together during the ball had given him such hope.

And if he was very, very fortunate indeed, maybe she could return his feelings.

His heart surged with joy at the thought of sharing Pemberley with Elizabeth, of building a life and a family together. So much of his first impression of her had been miscalculated, and he regretted wasting that time when he could have used it instead to get to know the real Elizabeth Bennet.

But the past was the past. He had learned from his mistake and would not make the same one again. He would earn her good opinion if it took the rest of his days, for there would be no other for him now that his heart was set.

He might be a stubborn man, grounded in his ways, but he was also steadfast and loyal to those he loved, and he was confident that he could make her happy if only she would allow him the chance to do so.

Resolved, Darcy strode to the table upon which the book rested and set down his candleholder.

His heart sprinting at an alarming speed, he lifted the volume and held it aloft by the leather spine, feeling along the edge of the pages until his finger located a narrow gap, its slim opening formed by paper not bound with the rest. With a mix of joy and trepidation, he sat in a nearby chair and spread the book open across his lap, lifting out a small bundle of folded foolscap.

The handwriting was, as expected, neat and lovely, with feminine loops and curls. It was also tiny, and Darcy knew instantly he would struggle to read in the inadequate light emanating from his single candle. Nevertheless, read he would. And what began as an errand to help a woman he'd come to adore, evolved entirely into something else as his eyes raced over some of the most intriguing sentences he'd ever read.

There was a greater number of pages than first he'd thought, and when finally he looked up from them to gaze at the grandfather clock with bleary eyes, he saw the first hint of daylight peeking through at the drape-covered edges of the library's tall windows.

"My God," Darcy whispered to himself as he carefully folded the precious papers and tucked them gently into a pocket of his robe, before pulling the garment more tightly around his torso.

The woman who held the key to his heart was also a magnificent storyteller.

He could not say that he was surprised, but the beauty and intelligence of her prose, and the energy and captivating pace of her plot were even superior to what he had imagined. Billings would no doubt find himself pleased beyond measure, and Darcy was certain the publisher would offer Elizabeth compensation which would provide a decent level of comfort—Lord forbid— should her mother and sisters ever lose their home and what he assumed would be a modest income.

Though, if his own hope came to fruition there would be no need for her to secure financial independence, as he planned to make her mistress of Pemberley, to share in all he possessed.

He closed the book and stood, returning the volume to the shelf where it belonged, then stopped at the table to retrieve his nearly-expired candle before slipping quietly through the library doors and out into the deserted hallway.

Soon the household staff would begin to stir, but he had a while to make it back to his room before his valet arrived to light the fire and begin readying things for the day ahead.

And it would be a full day indeed. He would not delay in contacting Billings, never mind that it was the first day of the new year and the publisher would likely be at home with his family. If his father's old friend would agree to meet with him, Darcy would see to it that the man's time was duly recompensed.

He was beginning to realize that he would do anything for his Elizabeth.

"Why, dear brother, you look exceedingly tired this morning," Georgiana noted, as Darcy entered the morning room.

His sister smiled brightly at him from the sideboard, where she had just picked up a plate. She wore a new gown in a deep green shade that he had given her for Christmas, and he was pleased to see that it complimented her coloring quite well. The seamstress at Georgiana's favorite shop had been most helpful in the choice, and Darcy made a mental note to stop in soon to express his gratitude.

"I am sure you are not wrong," he said, grinning. "I had some trouble sleeping last night."

"I am very sorry to hear that," she answered, placing a

few sausages alongside her eggs. "I did not sleep very well, myself," Georgiana continued, scrunching up her nose in the endearing way she had since she was in the nursery. "I believe I was too excited after the festivities."

Though they were siblings, Darcy's young sister was in many ways more like a daughter to him, due to the number of years separating the two. He had put much of his heart into caring for her since the death of their beloved parents, and, while he knew he could never replace them, and he had certainly made mistakes, he hoped he had at least shown Georgiana how much she was loved.

He studied her now—her golden hair and fair skin flaunting the glow of youth even after a late party, whereas he probably looked about as appealing as something a cat might drag in from the stables.

"You might be fatigued, sister, but it does not show," he said, filling his own plate as she finished with hers and headed to the table. He followed shortly after and took a seat, motioning to the footman for tea.

"That is good to hear," she said, after taking a sip of her own. "I am to visit Sarah this morning, and I wish to look well." Color gathered at the peaks of her cheekbones.

Darcy's next breath stuttered slightly at the mention of Georgiana's oldest friend. Her oldest friend who had a brother two years her senior...a young man for whom Darcy was beginning to believe Georgiana carried a special fondness. He had seen his sister dance with Henry the night before, and she sat next to him at dinner.

Had Darcy's own mind not been quite so thoroughly occupied with a pair of fine eyes, he might have paid closer attention and made an effort to speak with the lad to make him feel especially welcome in their home. If Georgiana did indeed have affection for her friend's brother, Darcy would encourage the match; he longed to see her happy and Henry was a kind, smart fellow from a good and warm family.

"Ah, I see," Darcy said, fidgeting with his napkin.

At times like these, the lack of feminine influence in their home was acutely apparent. He wished, not for the first time, that he had a partner by his side as he navigated raising a young woman.

"Well, give them my best."

Georgiana's fork paused midair and her mouth formed a wide grin, which he returned. "I will do that, Fitzwilliam, thank you," she said, the dimples in her cheeks giving away her obvious pleased that her choice met with his approval.

Her near-elopement with Wickham was in the past, and Darcy sensed that his sister was eager to move along with life and put that dreadful incident behind her.

After they had shared breakfast and more lighthearted chatter about who had danced with whom at the ball, Darcy reached into his coat and pulled out the pages that Elizabeth had left in his library the night before.

Georgiana's brow furrowed as she swallowed a bite of egg and glanced over. "What is that?" she asked, with only slight interest.

Darcy could not hide his excitement. "I would like for you to read these pages and tell me what you think."

"Alright," she answered, drawing out the word with surprise. "Aren't you going to tell me what they are first?"

"Just read," he insisted. "Then we will discuss the contents."

He motioned for another cup of tea and sipped in silence, hardly able to endure his impatience while his sister's eyes scanned the pretty penmanship. When Georgiana briefly looked up after what felt like hours, he forced his features into a normal expression so as not to influence her opinion.

"What do you think?" he asked, sounding too eager even to his own ears.

His sister's eyes were wide and her smile broadened as she folded the papers she had already read. When he reached for the rest, he thought she might clobber him.

"Not so fast," she warned, bending closer over the foolscap, ready to return to the story once he ceased pestering her. "Whatever this is, it's…it's wonderful. Who wrote this?" She waved a hand over the unfinished story.

"Miss Elizabeth Bennet," he answered, feeling very proud to know the bearer of that name.

Georgiana's face lit with recognition. "The lovely lady to whom you introduced me last night, who then sat between us at dinner?"

"The very same," Darcy said, hiding an overzealous grin behind his teacup. He did not want to alarm the poor girl. "That is not the whole of the book, I imagine, but you can see as well as I that she is a very talented authoress."

"Talent does not begin to cover it," his sister muttered as she flipped through the remaining pages. "It is positively riveting. I dread coming to the end of what you have here because I fear the story will not yet be resolved,

and I cannot wait to get hold of the rest. Do you
have more?"

Darcy shook his head. "I do not. Not yet. But I plan to
change that very soon."

"How?" Georgiana asked, leaning toward him. "Does
Miss Elizabeth plan to publish this story?"

Darcy hoped his face did not flush. "I do not know," he
said truthfully, "but I plan to help her if she does."

His sister's bemused expression prompted him to
explain further.

"I am taking this to Father's old friend, Mr. Billings,
this very day. He is a publisher of some renown, and the
only person I trust to offer fair compensation for what I am
certain will become a bestselling novel, if Miss Elizabeth
agrees."

"And what if she will not?" Georgiana asked, worry
lacing her tone. "Or what if Mr. Billings will publish, but
only if Miss Elizabeth makes changes."

She put a hand to her forehead. "Oh, I do hope he will
leave it as is. I have fallen quite in love with Thomas and
Meera, and I want to see them wed as adamantly as their
parents are against it. I cannot rest until I find out if they
will escape their families in India and catch the ship to
America. The story is perfect as is, and I will not hear a
harsh word against it!"

Darcy chuckled at his sister's vigorous defense of a
book he loved just as much.

"I would accept nothing less," he assured her. "Though
when Billings reads this, I am sure he will react in much
the same way that we did." His tone turned serious. "I do
hope Miss Elizabeth will not object. I would very much

love to surprise her with an offer of publication and see her hard work rewarded. Her novel deserves to be read by others, and will delight even the most discerning readers, I am sure."

Georgiana studied her brother. "Are you certain this is the best path—surprising her with the news, I mean?"

Her eyes softened. "I can see that you are enamored of Miss Elizabeth, brother. I would be a fool not to have noticed the extent of your enjoyment in her company at dinner last night, or the way you could not take your eyes off hers while dancing."

"It is that obvious, is it not?" he asked rhetorically, no longer caring if anyone saw how glad the woman made him. He had waited long enough to find someone with whom to spend the rest of his life, and once the decision had been made, he had no desire to hide his feelings.

He prayed this plan would earn her favor.

"I have thought much on this, and—yes—I believe it is the best way. When I encountered Miss Bennet and Miss Elizabeth at Hatchards, the elder could not say enough about how much this book meant to her, and I know now, having read it myself, that her enjoyment of it was not influenced by their sisterly bond. It is genuinely excellent, and I am sure no one has ever given Miss Elizabeth such a gift. A contract, and the career that I firmly believe would follow, would mean security and independence for her, and the freedom to choose the sort of life she wishes, regardless of whether she marries or not."

That last bit stung a little, but Darcy meant every word. He would do this for her even if she did not choose him after all.

He had caused Miss Elizabeth and her sister pain, and then he had seen the error of his way and fallen quite in love with her. Now he would prove that love, even if it was not returned.

"You do wish to see her married, though, do you not?" Georgiana asked, her voice full of fondness for her only sibling. "Indeed, I believe you have someone in mind."

"I never could hide my true feelings from you," he said. "You have always seen right through me."

"You never hesitate to return the favor," she replied. "You even intuited enough to save me from Wickham."

Her eyes clouded briefly—not, Darcy thought, with regret, but rather with relief that she had narrowly avoided sailing headlong into a storm she would not have survived.

"Would you be pleased?" he asked. "To have such a sister-in-law?"

Georgiana stood from the table and came up behind his chair, encircling her arms around his shoulders. "I would love nothing more," she answered, "than to see you happy. And that I should gain such a lovely sister at the same time, is only an added blessing."

CHAPTER 9

Two days later, Jane and Elizabeth were playing with their young cousins when a footman entered the nursery, carrying the morning post atop a silver tray.

The sisters glanced at each other with shared joy. Elizabeth hoped to hear from her friend, Charlotte, and Jane was expecting a letter from Longbourn with all the familial news of home.

Neither was prepared for what actually arrived.

Elizabeth put down the doll she'd been helping the little girls to dress for a make-believe tea party, as the footman neared to deliver a folded sheet of paper sealed in wax. Jane glanced up from where she had been exerting great effort to keep the boys from fighting over a rowdy, probably ill-advised, indoor game of *jeu de volant*.

When Elizabeth's hand flew up to cover her mouth, Jane grabbed the rackets from both boys and bid them quiet down immediately; they did so, shocked that their usually very docile cousin was capable of speaking so firmly.

Jane waved over the footman. "Please summon the governess back from her break with my apologies," she whispered, though Elizabeth still heard. "My sister and I must quit the nursery."

As soon as Sarah arrived to resume her duty of minding the children, Jane took Elizabeth by the arm and led her to their guest bedroom.

By the time they arrived, and her sister helped settle her onto a sofa, Elizabeth was feeling even more confused than when she'd just finished reading the letter. She was glad her aunt and uncle were out shopping that afternoon, as she did not wish for an audience apart from Jane.

"Lizzy, please tell me right away what is wrong," Jane insisted, her voice shaking with worry. "You are dreadfully pale."

Elizabeth shook her head, but still she could not seem to focus. She sat silent for a long moment as Jane continued to fret. "I am not sure I can explain it to you, sister, when I cannot quite understand it myself."

Jane's brow furrowed and Elizabeth wondered if it wasn't she who should be comforting Jane, and not the other way round.

"Do try," Jane pressed.

Elizabeth closed her eyes and pulled in a deep breath to steady herself. "Alright. I shall do my best."

Jane nodded and Elizabeth felt her sister's fingers wrap around her own.

"It is a letter from a London publisher," she began, then paused. She had hoped one day she might say the words she was about to utter, but certainly not under such circumstances. "He wants to publish my book."

At this news, Jane's eyes widened and her mouth spread open with cheer. Elizabeth felt her hand being squeezed within an inch of its life.

"Oh, Lizzy, this is wonderful news," Jane said. "The most wonderful news, indeed." She stopped speaking for a moment, presumably as she allowed it all to settle in her mind. "This is what you have wanted for so long. It is like a dream come true!"

Elizabeth tried very hard not to shake her sister. "Yes, it is what I've wanted," she nearly shouted, grimacing when she saw the effect her raised voice had on her sweet sibling. "But do you not see, Jane?" She held out the letter and shook it instead. "I did not even send my book to anyone. It is not yet even finished."

Jane frowned, a rare sight. "I do not understand," she said. "I assumed you may have done so in secret a few days hence, but if you did not send it in, then who?"

"I cannot be certain yet, though I have an idea," Elizabeth muttered through clenched teeth.

Jane's nodded rapidly with insistence that her sister continue.

"Do you recall two nights ago at the ball, when I ventured into Mr. Darcy's library for some time?" Elizabeth asked.

"Yes, of course. You indicated that all went according to plan."

"Well, I believe I left part of my manuscript in the book I used there for research." Elizabeth sighed and put her head in her hands. "I have not missed it since, as I was too distracted with what happened between…between Mr. Darcy and I…and I have not written anything these last two days."

"Yes, alright," Jane said. "You were taken by surprise when Mr. Darcy showed such kindness; it is not difficult to understand that, in your state, you quite forgot your reason for being there in the first place and left your things behind. But how, then, did they end up in the hands of a publisher?"

Elizabeth bit her lip as she locked eyes with her sister. "I believe Mr. Darcy may have found my pages, and, well…brought them to this"—she held out the offending letter—"publisher."

Realization flooded Jane's countenance. "Oh," she said. "Now I understand."

"Then, surely, you understand as well why I am so distraught," Elizabeth said, peering over the letter once more to be sure that it was real.

"Oh, Lizzy," Jane said, clicking her tongue. "Can you not overlook the way this came about, in favor of seeing the benefit?" She squeezed her sister's hand again. "Your book—your wonderful, wonderful book—will be published! All of England will read it and fall in love with your writing as I have, and I have no doubt the publisher will offer you a nice sum to proceed forward, once you accept a meeting with him."

Jane gently pried away the letter and read it herself, which did not take long. As Elizabeth knew from reading it again just a moment before, it was very brief, indicating only that Mr. Billings had received the pages and enjoyed them so much that he immediately wished to see more, requesting that Elizabeth visit his office in town as soon as possible.

It did not say from whom the publisher had obtained the portion of her manuscript, but there was only one explanation for that.

"No," Elizabeth answered. "I cannot overlook such a transgression, not after all Mr. Darcy has already done to harm you, and offend me."

Jane's eyes beseeched her. "But I thought you said that he had apologized for what he'd done and even planned to speak with Mr. Bingley about his affection for me. Indeed, when we spoke at the ball, Charles promised to send word to Father of his intentions, in lieu of going to Longbourn himself in such disagreeable weather. I expect to hear from him any day, as soon as Father responds."

"Oh, Jane, he did apologize." Elizabeth spoke in a rush. "That is precisely why this letter is so vexing. Do you still not comprehend my way of thinking? He has betrayed my trust by taking this letter to a publisher without asking my permission—when it is not even finished, for heaven's sake!"

"Perhaps that only means Mr. Billings perceives how truly marvelous the book is, and he wants to be the first to offer publication before any others catch wind of it," Jane suggested in a soothing tone.

In the back of her mind, a tiny voice whispered that her sister might be correct, but Elizabeth was so angry at Mr. Darcy for taking such action without consulting her, that she could not at present see past the dark fog of her fury.

Pushing her shoulders back and standing so quickly from the chair that it wobbled a little, Elizabeth braced herself. "Mr. Darcy has a great deal of explaining to do," she said, as she walked to the door, leaving behind a bewildered Jane. "That is, before I refuse ever to speak to him again."

After receiving the letter and talking with Jane, Elizabeth had attempted a walk out of doors to sort through the thoughts chasing each other across her mind, only to return after less than half an hour. The cold, like her heart, was simply too bitter to tolerate, and she had thus retreated to her room with a request not to be disturbed for the remainder of the day.

She knew her reclusive behavior was rude, especially as she and Jane would be leaving as soon as the weather cleared enough for them to return to Longbourn. Spending time with her aunt, uncle, and cousins was the proper thing to do—not begging off sick to sulk in her room.

Jane was a dear not to verbalize that very thought; no one would have blamed her for admonishing Elizabeth to come downstairs and socialize, but she did not wish to be talked out of her bad mood.

Mr. Darcy was wrong to share her book without asking first! She was sure of it.

For the most part.

At least when she was not reading and re-reading the publisher's letter over and over, still quite in doubt of its veracity. She had scanned the few sentences so many times that she'd memorized them, a fact she would admit to no one, not ever. She had resolved herself to remain angry with Darcy because of what he had done this time, and it would not do if Jane discovered her secret: that a part of her was excited beyond words that a publisher—a real, live, London publisher—had requested to see the whole of her novel, with design to turning it into a book that would be displayed on store shelves for purchase by living, breathing readers.

Oh, it was so hard not to let her mind run away with such imagining…walking back into Hatchards in the future to find her own story sitting there amongst her favorites. No one would know her true name, of course, but that hardly mattered—because Elizabeth would know. She would know it was hers, and she would run her finger along the spine, and…

"Lizzy," Jane said, causing her sister to jump a half-inch off her chair by the waning fire.

Pulled quite abruptly from the reverie she should not have allowed in the first instance, Elizabeth's cheeks warmed as she caught the trace of a grin on Jane's lips. Her sister paused just inside the door and tilted her head, and a very unladylike curse passed through Elizabeth's mind at the reminder that she could not hide her innermost thoughts from her eldest sibling.

"You were thinking about the offer, were you not?" Jane asked, striding closer.

Elizabeth pulled her wrap tighter around her shoulders. "Thinking about what?" she asked, feigning innocence. "I know not of what you speak."

Jane sat in a chair on the other side of a small table that separated the two. "Nonsense," she said. "You were imagining what it would be like to cease this ridiculous pouting and allow Mr. Billings to publish your book."

Elizabeth's mouth involuntarily opened and closed again, making her feel rather like a trout. "I was not," she argued, crossing her arms.

Jane rolled her eyes, but Elizabeth noticed that there was something different about her sister—a glow emanated from her as if she had swallowed the sun.

"Never mind me," Elizabeth said, leaning closer to inspect Jane's features. "What has gotten into you?"

Jane's entire being practically erupted with happiness; it spilled out of her presence with such exuberance that, despite her terrible mood, Elizabeth could not keep herself from mirroring Jane's smile.

"I do not wish to ignore your plight, Lizzy, but I have such wonderful news; I cannot keep it to myself a second longer."

"Then do not, sister," Elizabeth said, reaching over to grasp Jane's hands. Like their owner, they were warm, regardless of the lingering chill in the room.

Jane paused, holding the news within herself just a moment longer before speaking it aloud. "It is just that Mr. Bingley has…he has proposed marriage!" She took a breath. "To me, Lizzy!"

"Tell me everything. I want to know exactly how it transpired." Elizabeth's heart overflowed, and she forgot her own feelings as she shared in her sister's fervent joy.

"It was magical, just magical." The words rushed out of Jane on a river of bliss. "I could hardly breathe when he revealed that he has loved me all along, and that he never should have allowed Mr. Darcy to convince him that I did not share his feelings."

Indeed, he should not have, Elizabeth thought but did not say aloud.

"But they have been friends for so long, and I imagine it would be much the same if you had said something similar to me. He felt he had no choice but to trust his friend. And he did say, in Mr. Darcy's defense, that Mr. Darcy truly believed I did not feel the same as Charles at the time, and that he was only trying to keep him from getting his heart broken. Oh, it was all nothing but a dreadful misunderstanding, which has since been sorted."

At this, Elizabeth nodded. Charles' account mirrored Mr. Darcy's, and she was very glad that Jane had received the happy ending she deserved.

"But he does love me after all, Lizzy, and he has done so since first we danced. He asked if he could have the privilege of making me happy as we grow old together. He has written to Father to ask his blessing, and I have no doubt that he will receive it tenfold. I cannot even imagine what Mama will say."

Jane leaned back in her chair and breathed a sigh of pure contentment.

Then she paused and peered at her sister with uncharacteristic intensity, quite alarming Elizabeth.

"What is it?" Elizabeth asked, her merriment over Jane's engagement subsiding in the shadow of her sister's suddenly solemn expression.

"Mr. Darcy was here with Charles, you know," Jane began hesitantly. "I told him gently, out of Uncle's and Aunt's hearing, that it was probably best he call another day. I explained that you are not feeling well—in light of recent, unexpected news—and I believe he understood my meaning."

Jane studied Elizabeth's face carefully. "Was I wrong to turn him away?"

"No, no," Elizabeth answered. "You were quite right."

"It is only that I know how strong-willed you can be when you are angry, and I did not wish to see him hurt." Jane wrung her hands. "Though, in the end I was the one to cause harm. He seemed so eager to see you, and when I discouraged him, he looked as though he had lost all hope." She seemed a little guilty at this admission. "After all, whether it was right or wrong for him to go forth without first seeking your approval, he did do a kindness for you, Lizzy. He obtained for you something that you may never have been able to achieve on your own."

Elizabeth glared at her sister.

"I mean nothing by it, dearest. Only that…we are women; opportunities to find success in work we enjoy, without the judgment of our peers, do not abound for us. You know that better than anyone."

Jane waited, gathering her next words as the former began to settle on Elizabeth's heart.

"Perhaps Mr. Darcy was only trying to help you realize your grandest dream because he believes in you. Perhaps he even loves you, sister."

When Elizabeth looked up into Jane's eyes, tears began to form in her own, and she rubbed them quickly away with the back of her hand.

"Forgive me, Jane, but I believe I require a little time on my own to think this through," she said, offering a soft smile of reassurance. "You know I adore your company, but you have brought some things to my attention that I must ponder in private."

She breathed a deep sigh, letting her shoulders loosen for the first time since she had received the letter. "I fear I may have overreacted, and I need to decide what to do next."

Jane nodded, her sympathy palpable. "Take all the time you need, dear. I will tell our aunt and uncle that you are suffering a headache and will take your supper here."

"Thank you, Jane," Elizabeth whispered, reaching forward to embrace her greatest ally. "I do not wish to imagine what sort of mess I would have turned out to be, if I had not been born after such an excellent sibling."

Jane grinned and brushed a hand over Elizabeth's curls. "It is fortunate then that you do not have to find out."

Something dawned on her and Elizabeth frowned. "You will not allow your Charles to take you very far from me, will you? I do not know how I could survive at Longbourn without you. Mama and the girls are not the most suitable companions for me."

Jane's features softened with affection. "Of course I will not go far. And, if I may say, I do not believe it will come to pass that you will be long at home without me anyway."

CHAPTER 10

Reeling from Elizabeth's refusal to see him when he had called at Gardiner House the day prior, Darcy could not find peace.

Over and over, he reviewed the events of the past few days, until he thought at last that he might lose his mind. Finally, he decided that the only way to learn why she had rebuffed him after they had shared what he'd thought the finest evening of his life, was to ask her himself.

After they had opened their hearts to one another, and he had gone to Billings to seek publication for his beloved's first novel as a gift to her, he had hoped to propose marriage.

It would have been an evening of such merriment, securing a future with the woman he loved, even as his oldest friend did the same. He and Charles would have been brothers, and, he had believed, would have been the two happiest men in all of England.

But alas, something had altered in Elizabeth since last

they'd spoken, and he had the terrible idea that perhaps he had once again misjudged her sentiment where he was concerned. Though much had changed within his own heart, he reminded himself that he could not yet be certain if the same could be said for hers.

It was with all of that weighing heavily on his heart and mind that Darcy decided to call again at Gracechurch Street, never mind Elizabeth's initial rejection; he would demand to be seen…except doing so would require that the lady was in fact at home, and he discovered quickly that such was not the case.

"I am terribly sorry, sir," the butler informed him as he stood in the hall of Gardiner House. "She has gone out, accompanied by a member of the staff, of course, to a bookstore."

"In this dreadful cold?" Darcy asked, shaking his head as he prepared to leave.

The butler nodded. "Would you like to leave a card, sir?"

Darcy replied that the courtesy was not necessary under the circumstances, and headed immediately back out into the frigid air. He knew exactly where she would be found, and he did not hesitate to follow her.

It had been his fault the first time, but he simply would not stand losing her again.

Elizabeth was loitering in the poetry section of Hatchards, the shop deserted on such an awful day so that she was rewarded with the privacy and quiet she craved.

Perhaps one day, Uncle Gardiner's footman would forgive her for requiring his services that afternoon, when persons possessing more logic and reason than she had opted to stay indoors. As she watched him standing nearby, she imagined what he might be thinking—why could she not read all the same back at Gracechurch street.

But she could not.

Incessant thoughts about Darcy would not leave her, and, despite her hopes, they had followed her all the way to the bookshop. She was beginning to surmise that they might follow her for the rest of her life. It was likely she would never forget such a man.

Those penetrating dark eyes and the way they stared right into her heart. That dark hair that she could not help but imagine running her fingers through in a moment of passion. Those broad shoulders and strong arms that might embrace her, should she ever gain the courage to tell him how she truly felt…

But it would not come to pass.

Instead, she stood alone, in a drafty corner of a shop, reading something utterly wretched. How dare they—poets who had known true love—force their melodramatic emotions onto the public, when unsuspecting readers might wander upon their musings while nursing wounded hearts.

It was cruel behavior indeed, Elizabeth grumbled to herself as she slammed together the covers of the thin volume and shoved it back amongst its mates upon the shelf. Perhaps a history tome would prove a better balm to her foul mood.

She had turned to head toward that very section when

she saw something that made her sore heart stop altogether…

It was *him*. Standing there across what seemed a great chasm but was really only a few yards.

A few days hence, they had sat so close together that their knees touched—a sensation she would never forget—yet now she felt so very far apart from him.

Elizabeth was no longer angry, but she knew not how to say what she felt.

Jane had been right; she had been too hasty in her judgment of Darcy for submitting her book to Billings. And she had chastised herself relentlessly when she'd realized that what he had done had been a true gift. Maybe he had gone about it not in the best way, but from what she had witnessed of his character at the ball, he had meant well.

Nobody was perfect, least of all her.

They had both blundered in their assessment of one another, and now she wished only to make amends and tell him what was in her heart: she loved him.

She had protested too much when first he declined to dance with her at Netherfield, and now she knew exactly the reason. His rejection of her at that ball had stung precisely because she had been drawn to him, despite what she had thought to be pride and arrogance. And, quite the opposite, his reception of her at his own ball, and his admission of error regarding the first instance, had revealed to her his true character.

He had changed. He had listened to her and opened his heart to her. He had accepted her correction of his behavior and made adjustments accordingly. And beside all of that, when they had spoken together in that library, the warmth of the fireplace no match for the electricity that sparked between them, she had experienced the first inklings of love for him.

It had only grown in his absence, even as she'd raged over his attempt to please her.

And he had illustrated his honor by keeping his promise to rectify the relationship between Mr. Bingley and her sister. He was, by all accounts, a good man—one with whom she could now envision spending the rest of her life.

Except that it was too late.

Wasn't it?

"Elizabeth," Darcy said, reaching out a hand without moving his body any closer. He hesitated as though he did not know what to say next.

"Darcy," she answered, unable to form any other words of her own.

"I"—he paused, then seemed to resolve something within himself, and moved in her direction—"I have much I would like to say to you, if you will be so kind as to offer me a moment of your time."

She nodded, still at a loss for words, and he directed her to the fireplace, close to where they had stood and spoken tense greetings not so very long ago, when her feelings had been so different than they were now.

"Mr. Darcy, I have things I would like to say to you as well." Her voice quivered and she swallowed back the lump forming in her throat.

"Please, Elizabeth."

Her name on his lips did unsettling things inside her chest, and she breathed deeply to counter the effect.

"Allow me to speak first, as I am the one at fault for what has caused your recent anger toward me," he insisted.

She wanted to argue, but the eagerness to hear what he would say took precedence; thus, she simply nodded.

"Upon calling yesterday at your uncle's home, I received word from your sister that you were not feeling well due to, as she stated, unexpected news. After some thought, I surmised from her words that you had caught wind of Mr. Billings' devotion to publish your novel after seeing the portion of it that you left in my library. And, well, I confess I am as surprised as you are that Billings would have contacted you directly." He raised his palms in submission. "I fully expected to hear from him first myself. He must have been so thrilled with your work that he could not wait to make you an offer, and the situation quite escaped my grasp."

He reached forward, but stopped, closing his palms. "I am so very sorry."

Darcy's eyes pleaded with her. "I never intended to read your work without your permission. However, after we spoke and danced and dined together that night, I could not sleep for the idea that I had missed something. It was then that, leaving my bed, I remembered that you had been writing when I discovered you in the library. As far as what transpired after, I can only say that something overcame me, and I had to know what you had written."

As he verbalized the things he had been holding inside, Elizabeth knew what her response would be, but longed to know more about the decisions he'd made. She wanted to hear, in his own words, why he had gone out of his way to ensure that her book would be published.

She struggled to maintain even breaths, but she nodded and bid Darcy continue.

"I wanted to know you better, you must understand." He paused to take a deep breath. "Please allow me to say that, as I have come to know you more intimately, I have discovered that you far surpass any first impressions I had of you."

His eyes softened as Elizabeth's own filled with moisture.

"As to why I then brought your pages to Mr. Billings, I want you to know that my only aim was to assist you in achieving what I already knew you deserved. I wanted to show you that I was truly remorseful of my actions, which separated Bingley and your sister, and more importantly, I wished to prove that your work is excellent and that others should have the privilege to enjoy it, as I have."

She brought a handkerchief to her eyes and dabbed at the liquid. "And you are so certain that they will?" she asked. "Enjoy my work."

"Strong faith in one's convictions is not always a bad thing," Darcy answered, grinning mischievously. "Especially when one is right."

She could not help but smile. "I understand why you did this," she said softly. "But you see, I wanted to succeed on my own merit." She looked straight into his eyes, hoping he could understand. It was not easy to explain a woman's hurdles to a man of name and means.

"I do see," he said, and she believed him. "But if I cannot use my position in society to lift up your work when it is so commendable of its own accord, then what good am I?"

Oh, how close she had come to a life without Darcy. Surely he could not say anything to make her love him more.

"You are wise beyond your years, keen of thought, and sharp of tongue, which—I fear I must admit—I enjoy to no end. I love you, Elizabeth, and I wish only for your true happiness. I will do anything in my power to secure it."

And yet he had already done exactly that.

She could scarcely speak. Her heart was full to bursting and she worried that if she said anything at all, or merely moved an inch, this would all turn to dust and she would wake up in her bed at Longbourn, realizing it had all been just a dream.

But he stared at her as though her next words held the weight of the world, so she would try.

"So, Mr. Darcy, am I to understand that your first impression of me has altered, and I am now handsome enough to tempt you?" she asked, teasing him.

What he did next would have caused her to faint, if she had been the fainting sort. But he was right about her—she was nothing if not a force to be reckoned with—and when he took her hand, removed her glove, and wrapped the exposed flesh of his fingers around her own, Elizabeth merely smiled and held on tight.

"Dearest Elizabeth—not only are you more than handsome enough to tempt me every day for the rest of my life—you are enough of everything, in every way, to drive me to madness should I be denied the privilege of your hand, or of always, always being your very first reader."

"Then, Mr. Darcy," she said, "I must tell you that I love you, as well. And I shall not deny you any longer."

He leaned in close, and she felt the whisper of his breath against her cheek, just before his lips touched hers in the first of many, many, blessed kisses.

EPILOGUE

When it arrived, the parcel was wrapped in unassuming brown paper, like any ordinary gift.

But this was not a simple pair of gloves, or a wrap to drape over her shoulders on a chilly winter's morn. Nor was it something finer, such as a string of pearls, or a token of similar value.

This was far grander than any of those things.

And when Elizabeth, with shaking fingers, pried away the paper, her heart fluttered in a way usually reserved for romance.

But this was also not romance.

This was the culmination of a dream.

Made of her own heart and mind, it was so much more than any normal gift, and yet, as she paused to enjoy the special moment, she relished the knowledge that it might not have been possible had she taken a different path, or failed to see behind the once prideful exterior of the man who helped bring it to life.

Tossing the parchment aside, Elizabeth lay the leather-bound volume upon her lap—not an easy feat with the way her abdomen had grown in anticipation of their first child —and opened the front cover.

The drawing room full of family and dear friends, there to celebrate with her on that memorable day, faded into the background. All she could see was the beautiful print on the second page, which held a tenderly composed message to the man who stood next to her, gazing into her eyes with a different sort of pride than she had encountered when first they'd met…

Her loving husband, Fitzwilliam Darcy.

Dear Reader,

Thank you so much for giving this story a try!

Reviews are very important to authors because they help readers find new books to enjoy. Whether or not you enjoyed this story, please consider leaving a review wherever you purchased the book.

If you would like to be the first to receive information on new releases, please sign up for my newsletter. Mailings are infrequent, and you are always welcome to unsubscribe if you wish to do so. Your email address remains private and will not be shared.

All the best from a very thankful author,

A.J. Woods

ABOUT THE AUTHOR

A.J. Woods has loved Jane Austen since her first reading of *Pride and Prejudice* in seventh grade. She has a degree in English Literature and enjoys movies and quality time with her family.

A.J. loves hearing from readers, and can be found at https://www.facebook.com/AuthorAJWoods.

45669970R00071

Made in the USA
San Bernardino, CA
31 July 2019